"You di

I listen

to glare up at him, and he could see every speck, every detail of the irises of her eyes, and the way the pupils changed.

"I'm not letting you out of here until you let me apologize." Though it nearly choked him to say it, it was the right thing to do.

Surprise covered her face for an unguarded second, and her pupils dilated at the rush of pleasure his words caused. When her lips parted, they drew his attention. If he were a different man, in a different situation, he wouldn't have hesitated to close the gap between them and find out how soft her lips were. If he were a different man he'd take her in his arms and press her length against his. But he wasn't, and he didn't. He couldn't.

Dear Reader,

Thank you so much for picking up a copy of *Socialite…or Nurse in a Million?* This is the second book I've set in the city where I live—Albuquerque, New Mexico. When I came to New Mexico for the first time as a travel nurse, I didn't fall in love with it right away, but found that I kept returning for more assignments and staying for longer periods of time.

At over five thousand feet above sea level, the desert here is high-altitude living. The textures, the colors, the scents are incredible—and very different from where I grew up. Each walk into the desert brings a new breathtaking sight. I've tried to infuse some of my love for the high desert into this book. It was a surprise to me that I fell so in love with the culture and landscape here, and I hope you'll enjoy exploring it with me.

Love,

Molly

SOCIALITE...OR NURSE IN A MILLION?

Molly Evans

Harlequin®

TORONTO NEW YORK LONDON
AMSTERDAM PARIS SYDNEY HAMBURG
STOCKHOLM ATHENS TOKYO MILAN MADRID
PRAGUE WARSAW BUDAPEST AUCKLAND

ISBN-13: 978-0-373-06778-7

SOCIALITE...OR NURSE IN A MILLION?

First North American Publication 2011

This edition published by arrangement with Harlequin Books S.A.

For questions and comments about the quality of this book please contact us at Customer_eCare@Harlequin.ca.

www.eHarlequin.com

Printed in U.S.A.

SOCIALITE...OR NURSE IN A MILLION?

This book is dedicated to health care workers
in the trenches, who get the job done every day.

CHAPTER ONE

Albuquerque, New Mexico, USA

VICTORIA Sterling-Thorne walked into the South Valley Healthcare Clinic and knew she looked as wide-eyed and green as a student nurse on her first day of clinicals, because that's exactly how she felt. That wasn't going to stop her, though. It was just nerves on the first day of a new job. That was all. She'd been through it in the past, and she'd get through it now. On this first day of May, it was the beginning of a new month and a new way of life for her. One she hoped would be an exciting chapter in her life and some great experience in her pocket. This clinic had a great reputation, and she wanted to be a part of it.

She chewed on her lower lip. Had she made the right choice by coming here, by not hiding who she was, changing the name that made people see dollar signs? The past had a strange way of casting its reflection forward, and she hoped that wasn't going to be the case now. Indecision made her stomach churn. With any luck she'd made the right decision, and it was too late to turn back now.

Although she was an experienced nurse, this was a

venture out of her comfort zone. Her father's chiding words and her brother's laughter still stung her pride. Determined to prove them wrong and, more importantly, to prove to herself that she could handle it, she had deliberately chosen this clinic far from her usual world of controlled, private hospitals and clinics. The mission statement here was closer to what her original goals in nursing had been. The time had come to make it happen.

For too many years she'd lived with the influence of her family hanging around her shoulders like a too-tight scarf she couldn't take off. Now she just wanted to be a nurse who took care of people. That's all.

She approached the glass door and opened it.

The clinic was packed with people. Some sat, some paced, some comforted small children, and they were all waiting for appointments. She'd never seen so many people lined up before a clinic even opened. That spoke silently of the great need of this community, but also of the quality of care they received there. Even though her nerves still tingled with anticipation, she knew this was the right move for her. She hadn't taken her career choice lightly when she'd entered nursing school despite the protests of her family, and she wasn't stopping now. Anyone who stood in her way could just get lost, including her family. Helping people who needed it gave her satisfaction that matched nothing else in her world. Somehow she saw parts of her mother in each patient she took care of. For her mother it had been too late, even before she'd been diagnosed. Cancer had invaded before she'd even known what had been wrong. Vicki wanted to help keep others from experiencing the same loss that had changed her life as a teenager. But this atmosphere was at complete odds with the type of hospital she had been working in for the past five years.

Looking around, she quickly found the nurses' station. "Hi, I'm Vicky, your new nurse." She hoped the woman remembered her from the interview last month.

A thin, gray-haired woman, who looked as if she might have known Florence Nightingale personally, peered up at Vicky over half-moon magnifier glasses. "Yes, Vicky Sterling-Thorne?" she asked in a cheerful and kindly voice.

"Yes. I prefer just Thorne, though. Makes the paperwork easier."

"Right. Just to refresh you, I'm Tilly McGee. Come on back, and I'll show ya round." She rolled her wheeled desk chair back and opened a side door for Vicky to enter. "As you can see, we've got a full docket today, so you may have to work on your own some, check vitals here and there, that sort of thing. Orientation could be a little unorthodox." She shook her head, as if knowing something that Vicky didn't.

"That's okay. I'll try to be helpful where I can. That's why I'm here." She turned and bumped into someone who had entered the station right behind her. "Oh, sorry." She looked at the handsome man, who took a step back from her. The blue scrubs failed to identify his status at the clinic. "Are you one of the nurses?"

A crooked smile crossed his face, and his deep brown eyes lit up for a second. "Some days I'm everything. Nurse, unit secretary, lab tech and clinic doctor all rolled into one." The smile he tossed her way was brief but welcoming.

Vicky blinked. "That's an impressive job description,"

she said, intrigued at his response. Here was a man who could multitask.

"It is." The welcoming smile faded away to what could only be an expression of mistrust. What had she done already to invite that? He sighed. "I guess you're the new nurse, aren't you?"

"Yes. You look disappointed already."

"I wouldn't call it disappointment."

Wariness stirred inside her. Had her family reputation preceded her so quickly? She gave a sigh of her own and hoped to head off any bias from the get-go. "My name is Vicky and, despite what you may think, I'm a nurse, that's all."

He nodded. "Just to let you know, quickly, our last nurse didn't return from maternity leave, and we've been shorthanded for weeks."

"The agency nurses worked for a while, but we need a full-time nurse, not a stopgap." Tilly grumbled her words without looking up from the computer.

Vicky nodded and gave a tight smile, understanding some of the man's reluctance. Despite the glowing references she had sent over, he had no confidence in her skills as a nurse. Time would change all that. "Well, I'm here to help. Where do we start?"

"Introductions, I guess." He glanced around. "Carlos is around here somewhere. He's the assistant extraordinaire, don't know what we'd do without him. And I'm Dr. Miguel Torres. We're not too formal, so call me Miguel."

Reluctantly, he stretched a hand out and shook hers in a firm but brief grasp. His hand was warm and not soft, like most of the men she knew who made money with their hands, but nothing else. The texture of Miguel's hand made her think he used his hands for building things and a slight shiver rocked her. She hoped that wasn't an omen. Work was her reason for being there and she hoped that she didn't have to remind herself that the boss was a hands-off relationship.

"Glad to be here."

Stepping back from her, Miguel glanced at the purse and lunch bag in her hands. "Tilly, can you set her up with a locker? By the look of that bag, she's going to need one."

She watched Miguel stride toward the triage area and wondered if there was anything behind that comment or was she just too wary of new people based on the experiences of her past?

"Come on, honey. I'll get you set up." The two women completed the task in a few minutes. Tilly returned to the desk to organize the patients, and Vicky noticed Miguel engaged in what looked like an urgent situation. He was trying to take a blue-faced baby from a young mother.

"He's not breathing, he's not breathing!" the woman cried, and clutched the infant more tightly, not knowing she was harming him further.

"Let's have a look," Miguel said, his soothing voice trying to gain control over the situation, but the anxiety of the mother was overwhelming.

Vicky rushed forward. Unable to interrupt the conversation, she leaned closer to the baby and blew a puff of air onto his face.

Startled, the infant jumped and took in a breath. And then another. And in seconds it turned from a ghastly blue to a lovely, normal shade of pink.

Openmouthed, the mother gaped at Vicky. Miguel

raised amused eyes at her and gave a surprised look. The situation lost its tension in just a few seconds.

"What?" she asked as she looked between them. Had she done something wrong already? Seemed as if she was always stepping in it somewhere, but she didn't want to do that her first day on the job. This was a job she wanted and needed. Messing up was not an option, no matter how much money her family had. It wasn't hers. She paid her own way based on her nurse's salary.

"What did you do to him?" the mother asked, her demeanor much calmer than it had been moments ago, though she still breathed rapidly.

"I just stimulated his breathing reflex. Something I learned in my first rotation in the nursery at my previous hospital." She gave Miguel a concerned look. "Once in a while newborns just forget to breathe, and if you blow a puff of air on their faces it startles them, and they take a breath. That's what baby reflexes are for." Vicky reached a hand out to the mother and patted her back in a soothing manner, trying to ignore the intense way that Miguel watched her, but the fluttering in her stomach wasn't going away. The intensity of him was going to take some getting used to. "Is it okay if we take a look now?"

"Yes, yes, yes. Dr. Torres, I'm so sorry!" Tears now poured down the mother's face as she relinquished the baby to Vicky.

"It's okay," Miguel said, and squeezed her shoulder. "We'll take a look and make sure everything is okay, just to be sure."

Vicky handed the baby boy over to Miguel and engaged the mother in small talk to help calm her down and give herself a moment to beat her nerves down. "What's your name?"

"Tina."

"Why don't you have a seat for a second? I'm sure that you're worn-out." Vicky guided her to a nearby chair.

"I am. I'm shaking." She rubbed her hands up and down her arms, as if she felt chilled from the experience. "I thought he was going to die."

"He's okay now." Vicky raised her eyes to Miguel, who gave her a reassuring nod, which calmed her own nerves a bit. Having such a strong team leader who didn't get ruffled was going to be a wonderful experience. "It's scary when babies do that, isn't it?"

"Yeah, it is. Still, I bet this boy's going to be a champ one day." He wrapped the baby up in the soft blue blankets and tucked him against his body, talking to the infant as if they were old friends.

Vicky tried not to stare. The man was gorgeous with those incredibly dark eyes of his and hair to match, but coupled with a smile and a soft voice when talking to a baby? Absolutely stunning. Nothing like the men she knew in her part of the world far away from this clinic. Something cramped inside her chest, maybe a long-lost hope or dream of having a family. Since her divorce two years ago she'd not allowed herself to dredge up those forgotten dreams. A man with a baby was an intoxicating sight, but she'd learned long ago that not every beautiful man had a heart to match. And not one could be taken at his word. She finally had to look away when Tina asked her a question.

Miguel had seen infants like this come and go since he had taken over the clinic a few years ago. Some stayed healthy and survived, some didn't. His hope was that when they grew up, none of them would succumb to the influence of gangs and drugs, like his younger brother, Emilio, had done, but he knew that was probably unrealistic. Emilio's death at the hands of a gang was one of the reasons he himself fought so hard for every child that entered his clinic. Each battle to save a life was a battle with a gang or disease and every one was a battle he intended to win. Death was not going to defeat him or take the life of his patients. Not if he could help it. Back then he hadn't had the skills to save his brother, but he was different now. One day, maybe some of his patients could get the education they deserved and would live long, healthy lives far away from the tragedies of life. If he had some small part in helping that happen, all the better. It would help pay back the debt of honor he owed. Family was everything, and he owed much to them.

With the infant sleeping in the crook of his arm, he knelt beside Tina. "He's okay now. You did the right thing by bringing him in. The nasal congestion should go away in a few days with some medication I'll give you, but if it doesn't, bring him back."

"Seriously?" She looked at him, her eyes wide with shock, and tears welled again in her eyes. "That's all it is?"

"Seriously." He patted her shoulder again and gave her a smile. "That's all it is."

With a nod, Tina accepted the baby back. By watching her, how she continued to look at his face, the way she stroked his cheek with her finger, she had certainly bonded well with him and that was half the battle with very young mothers.

"You'll be fine. You just need to rest a little more and worry a little less," Vicky said.

"Thank you. You don't know how much that relieves my mind." She let out a shaky breath and brushed away the tears. "I always think the worst."

"Me, too. That way, if it doesn't happen, then it's good, right?" Vicky said, and gave Tina an encouraging smile.

"You're right. I guess that's what I do, too."

"There are times you will need to think with your mind and not your heart, even though it's really hard. I learned that a long time ago. You can try that little trick I showed you if he decides to stop breathing again."

"I will. Thank you."

Miguel watched the exchange with interest, wondering what the princess of the Sterling-Thorne vineyards was talking about. Surely she'd never had to suffer a day in her life, so he couldn't understand her words. As he watched her, though, she seemed to genuinely believe what she was saying to the young mother. Somehow these two had found a common bond that allowed Tina to relax a little. So very different, light and dark, they were a visual contrast to each other. Miguel could see by simple observation that Vicky wasn't from this part of town. Knowing her family history, he imagined she lived in a castle with an ivory tower. But if she fit into the clinic, he didn't care as long as she was a good nurse, and that was the reason she was there. Most people with her financial status simply made charitable donations. What she was doing there in the flesh was anyone's guess. Right now, none of it mattered when he had a waiting room full of patients. People with real needs were why he was here.

"Did you come by yourself or is there someone here with you?" Miguel asked Tina, and stood, directing his gaze away from Vicky's distracting beauty.

"My mother is in the waiting room."

"That's good. Is she helping you out at all?" Vicky asked as she walked with them out to the front.

"Yes. She helps me every day. I don't know what I'd do without her."

"Why don't you bring him back in a few days so we can do a well-baby checkup?" Vicky asked, then paused with a quick glance at Miguel. "Sorry. I should ask first. Do you actually have a well-baby clinic or something here?"

"Yes, we actually have one," he said with a little starch in his voice. "We're really a full-service clinic, though it may not look like it. One day a week we have a nurse practitioner come in. I'm hoping to increase her clinic to two days a week, but for now it's just one." He touched the sleeping baby again and marveled at the softness of his skin. They started out so innocent.

Wariness eased into Vicky's eyes, but she spoke kindly to Tina. "Oh, good. I'll look forward to seeing this little guy again. Let's have Tilly make an appointment for you." Vicky smiled, looking up at Miguel for confirmation. He nodded, his voice suddenly stuck. When Vicky smiled, it went all the way to her eyes and the outer corners turned up, making him wonder what secrets lay in their dark blue depths. He stepped back and cleared his throat, surprised by the attraction that surfaced in him. Now was not the time to be attracted to a coworker. Especially not one with a background that was totally at odds with his. In his experience, that sort of situation never turned out right. "Go ahead. I think he's fine now. See if she can make your appointment for about a week from now."

"Okay." She turned with Vicky and released a tremulous sigh.

Miguel watched them go and then prepared himself for the next patient of the day.

CHAPTER TWO

"So, is that your typical emergency around here?" Vicky asked Miguel as she followed him down the hall and around the corner to the staff lounge, which looked as if it had once been a large closet.

"We really see anything and everything here," he said, and put two cups of water in the microwave. "Coffee?"

"Sure."

In minutes he had heated water for the both of them and as Vicky watched, he opened a jar of instant coffee, spooning an uncertain amount in each cup. Hiding a grimace, she accepted the offering from him.

"Here's to your first day." He sipped and then sat at the small table. "We've only got a few minutes before we have every room full, so I'll give you the orientation of how I do things as we go. It'll be easier that way, rather than just telling you about it."

"I learn better that way, too." Vicky sipped from the cup, anticipating a vile brew. She wasn't disappointed. She tryied to hide her revulsion then reached for the sweetener on the table. "I think this needs a little sugar."

Miguel chucked. "You're being too kind. It needs a lot

more than that, but my taste buds were nearly destroyed by residency. If you're wanting good coffee, you'll have to bring your own in a thermos or something. The coffee fund went away with the budget cuts."

The stuff was despicable beyond description. Reaching into her jacket pocket, she pulled out a pack of mints and popped one in her mouth, hoping that it would kill the taste. "Oh. No worries. I'll figure something out, but I hope you won't be offended if I don't drink this," she said, and started to pour it into the sink.

"Wait, I'll take it." Miguel reached for the cup.

The poor man. No coffee fund? Horrors. She thought a second about a friend who had a coffee delivery business. She was going to have to talk to him. "So, tell me some more about the clinic."

"Oh, right." In just a few minutes Miguel had given her the quick history of the clinic, how he had taken it over on the brink of closure and brought it to life again. "The really unfortunate part is that our grant money is ending and the city is uncertain whether they can find money for this place. The state of the economy has hit them, too." He tugged at the lapel of his lab coat, and his lips pressed together firmly for a second. "I'm working every angle I can but it's just not coming together yet. There's got to be something else that will help."

She could see the worry etched on his lean face. He put a lot of energy and probably his heart into this clinic. "What about having a fundraiser?"

"The only fundraiser I've held myself is a bake sale, and we can't have enough of them to fund the clinic. The community has put together some car washes, stuff like that, but it's just not going to be good enough for long-term funding."

"No, I mean a big fundraiser where people and corporations donate large amounts of money for tax deductions. That's the kind you need." She'd put together a few of them herself and knew what it was all about. At least that's how things got done in her family's world. Things just snapped into place when a Sterling-Thorne wanted something done. You called your wealthy friends for donations or put on dinners and gave everyone a good time for their money. Couldn't that be done in this community, as well? Though it was foreign to her, there had to be some common ground.

Miguel heaved a sigh that spoke of long frustration and Vicky sensed that she'd unwittingly brought up something she shouldn't have. "I'm sorry. I didn't know the clinic was in a bind."

"You couldn't know." He gave an unhappy smile. "We've fortunately had a benefactor for several years. He died last year and the family has decided not to continue his charity work. The city might come through, but maybe not. We won't know until July or so what they can do, when their budget is finalized."

Anger surfaced in her at the injustice. She'd just started there and now it was in danger of closing. "That's just wrong. Is this a historic building or something?" Vicky asked, wondering how she could help save this little clinic.

"Good idea, but no. It's not old enough to be considered of historical significance, so there's no help there either."

The door to the tiny lounge burst open and a young man popped his head through the doorway. "Chest-pain patient coming."

"Chest pain trumps everything else," Miguel said, and they rushed out the door.

They dashed into a patient room where the young man she assumed was Carlos had disappeared into. Miguel was a man of energy, each movement strong, self-assured and confident, even though the patient looked quite gray. Vicky gritted her teeth and prepared herself, immediately switching on the E.R. nurse in her. Now was not the time for nerves.

"Get the crash cart ready," he said, his voice low, "and then get a line in him. Two if you can manage it."

Tilly hurried into the room. "I've called 911 for transport."

"Thanks, Tilly," Miguel replied. "He's going to need hospital care for sure. We'll get him as stable as possible first."

"Code cart is ready, Doctor," Vicky said, after tugging the massive tool kit on wheels to the patient's bedside. "Do you want to start a nitro drip?" Knowing her emergency medicine drills by heart, she hoped that she could anticipate Miguel's needs, as he hadn't been able to do any orientation with her yet.

"Yes."

The other two in the room seemed to know their roles well. Carlos hooked up the heart monitor, which looked as if it had come from an old hospital supply house. It was practically an antique, but it worked, and that was probably all Miguel wanted out of it. Next, he applied the automatic blood-pressure cuff. Tilly inserted an IV with a sure hand and hooked up the nitro drip that Vicky had prepared.

"The medication we're giving you should ease your pain quite a bit," she said to the male patient, who appeared to be in his mid-sixties. With one hand, she adjusted the oxygen mask over his face. His breathing was shallow and grunting, which was extremely worrying. She glanced at the monitor, interpreting the squiggles immediately. "Looks like he's having an infarct right now."

Miguel also looked at the monitor then at Vicky with surprise at her precise interpretation. "You're right. Start a potassium drip and give him an amp of magnesium." Leaning over the patient, he said, "Try to slow your breathing down."

"I'll do the mag—you get the drip ready," Tilly said, and together they got the medications prepared and into the patient.

Soon they heard the sound of sirens. "I'll go and get them," Carlos said, and dashed to the door. Vicky called out vital signs now and then so Miguel didn't have to keep looking up at the monitor.

Miguel remained focused on the patient situation, not being distracted by the other activity. "Keep the fluids going, increase the nitro drip."

"Yes, Doctor," Vicky responded, and although her hands trembled slightly, she changed the setting on the IV pump to the next level. "I hope it opens his vessels a little. He needs better circulation than he's got."

"Agreed." Miguel hit the print button on the old monitor that hung on the wall and a segment of the ECG appeared on paper, which he tore off. "He's got some serious S-T segment changes."

"Should we send that strip with him to the hospital?" she asked, knowing that the E.R. doctor there might appreciate that additional information to compare with further ECG interpretations.

"Yes." He pushed the print button again and a second strip printed from the machine.

The E.R. crew arrived, following Carlos, and in just a few minutes they had the patient transferred to their stretcher and he was out the door.

Vicky took a few deep breaths and placed a hand on her chest. "Wow. That was something."

Miguel's lips compressed into a line momentarily then he nodded, as if conceding something. "That *was* something. A trial by fire on your first day. Good job, everyone."

A flush of pleasure pulsed through her. Compliments certainly were unexpected at this point, especially after some of his earlier comments. "Why don't I get the room ready for the next patient?" she asked. A few minutes alone would do her some good, and she hoped that her limbs would stop shaking. She hadn't been prepared for such an urgent situation on her first day.

"I'll get the next few patients lined up," Tilly said, and returned to the nurses' station.

"Sounds good." He stepped out the door with Tilly and after a glance back he paused. "I'll just wash up first," he said, and returned to the room.

This was usually the time she collected her thoughts, after the scary stuff was over. A time she could allow herself to mentally go over the situation, make sure she'd done everything she could have and settle her churning stomach.

Miguel cleared his throat and looked at her, then his glance bounced away. "You were fine, Vicky," he said, startling her. She hadn't realized that he'd finished and was standing so close to her.

"I always second-guess myself, you know? Did we do everything and do it right?"

"I do know, and that's good, not bad. Reviewing a situation with a team member is always good to do. Emergencies like that don't come through the door every day, so it can be a little nerve-racking."

"I'm just thankful I didn't forget anything in the middle of it all, you know?" She opened the top drawer of the code cart. "I suppose you have replacement medications somewhere?"

"In the med room. Tilly can show you where." Vicky stopped and looked up at him. He was a head or so taller than her, and she was pretty long and leggy. She wore her pale blonde hair in a swingy bob that just grazed her collar. She was trim and had the look of a runner. Her eyes were a startlingly clear blue, and she had a nearly flawless complexion. There was a small scar on her left cheek that he wouldn't have noticed had he not been so close to her. It was probably from childhood chicken pox or something. Without it, he would have called her delicate, but the mark saved her from being too perfect. At least on the outside.

And he wondered again what this woman, who came from nearly unprecedented wealth, was doing in his humble clinic. The monthly income from the family business could probably finance his entire clinic for ten years. It boggled his mind to see her behaving just like any other nurse he could have hired. Frankly, he'd been against hiring her, but due to desperate measures he'd given in and offered her the job. Tilly had supported the idea of hiring her, and though his instinct had protested, he trusted Tilly implicitly. Vicky had looked good on paper, but that didn't mean she could hold up under the kind of pressure they sometimes got in the clinic, though she certainly had today. He hadn't changed his opinion in a few hours. Only time would tell, but he didn't totally mistrust her.

"What's wrong?" She held his gaze, and nothing but curiosity swirled there. "You're looking at me strangely."

Miguel met her gaze and held it for a few moments before answering. "What are you doing here?"

"You hired me."

Frowning, he shook his head. That hadn't come out right. "I mean, what is someone from your background doing at a clinic like this? Shouldn't you be working at a private hospital somewhere?"

"I *could* doesn't mean I *should* or that I even *want to*."

The light in her eyes faded, and she stepped back a pace. A frown flitted across her face, but he supposed he'd surprised her by his question. He ignored the squirm that it caused in his stomach. He'd learned the hard way, too, that people were hardly ever what they seemed.

"On the surface things are different than they really are. You must know that."

Wariness appeared in her eyes and her lips compressed. "I see. You don't think I'm capable of handling this job despite my excellent references and my performance during the crisis we just went through?"

"I know you're capable of it, but I don't know why you want to do it. With your family background—"

"Forget my background. Please. I'm here for the same reason as you, Doctor. I'm here to help people who really need it, not putting ice packs on someone who's had too much plastic surgery." She huffed out a sigh.

"Seriously, what makes you want to do this kind of work?" That was the big question. What made anyone want to do this kind of work? He had his reasons, which were private, very personal, and he wasn't about to share them with Vicky.

"If you're through being prejudicial, I'd like to get back to work. Tilly can orient me for a while if you need a break from someone like me." She turned to leave the room.

"Listen, that's not what I meant." Dammit. He hadn't intended to have this conversation and now that he was it was coming out badly.

"I think it's exactly what you meant, Doctor." Pausing, she looked over her shoulder with a tight smile.

"Vicky, this isn't coming out right." He tugged on his lab coat and straightened it, giving himself a moment to think. "I simply don't understand why someone who has all the opportunities in the world would choose to settle for a small clinic in the middle of nowhere."

"Maybe I don't consider it settling. I consider it an opportunity to expand my knowledge and skill base as a nurse." She shrugged and the steam seemed to fade out of her. "In nursing, if you don't keep your skills up you get stale and forget things. I don't want to forget things."

He'd have to accept that at face value, because at the moment he could find no other obvious motivation. "That's true for doctors, as well." He flipped his stethoscope around his neck and shoved his hands into his pockets. "Guess I'll get out of your way and let you finish up."

"Won't take long now." Vicky flashed a look at her watch and gave a surprised laugh. It was a nice sound, and one he didn't hear often yet. "Wow. It's only eleven. Feels like it's quitting time already."

"I know that feeling of strange time passage when you're in the midst of a code or something." He'd had that feeling even before his residency. When he'd held his dying brother in his arms so long ago. That had been the first time, and he'd never forgotten it.

CHAPTER THREE

THE rest of the day passed by in a rush of patients, most with minor complaints, upper respiratory issues and someone who had flattened a finger with a hammer. She and Miguel reverted back to their professional roles after the short exchange in the patient room. There was safety in her role, and it was one she knew well. She'd performed it often.

In her family, she'd been forced to play a role that she'd been desperate to escape for years. There had been various reprieves during nursing school and her short marriage. Now that she lived in the caretaker's cottage on her family estate and not under her father's thumb, she had found some relief. Living under her father's roof again was not an option. Only by helping others who needed it and being a nurse did she truly escape the artifice of her family's reputation, which always seemed to be more important than she was. When she entered the family domain, she was once again Victoria Sterling-Thorne, name before nursing.

Nursing was too personal, they thought, too hands-on. Just donate money from a distance and be done with it was their philosophy, and she didn't agree with it. There was simply something within her that wouldn't allow her to do that. A sigh eased out of her. She wasn't going to fix them, and they weren't going to influence her any longer. So back to work for now was the only answer.

The clinic stopped taking new patients at 4:00 p.m., so they were out the door by five when the clinic officially closed.

"I gotta go, M. If I'm late for dinner again, my mother's going to have a fit." Carlos hefted a backpack over one shoulder.

Miguel smiled at the young man and nodded. "Get out of here. Tell her I said hello and it was all my fault."

"You've got it." Carlos strolled out the door and disappeared down the sidewalk into the early-evening shadows.

"Tilly, you ready to roll?" Miguel asked as other staff members filed out the door.

Tilly left the nurses' station and closed the door. "Yeah." She paused for a second, looking at Vicky, then directed a pointed glance at Miguel. "Good going, kid. See you tomorrow."

Vicky retrieved her purse from the locker and reveled in the tiny compliment that Tilly had given her. Although this was a new venture for her, she thought she might like it here. As she proceeded to the door, she realized that Miguel hadn't moved and she waited for him. "Aren't you coming?"

"I've got some notes to finish first," he said. "But I'll walk you out." He left the chart where it was and stood, but Vicky didn't move. She stayed rooted where she was, looking at him seriously, assessingly, making him a little curious as to what was going on in her mind. There was something about her that made him uncomfortable, and he had no idea what it was. He'd been around plenty of lovely women and many nurses before, so simple attraction wasn't the answer. Maybe it was the way her eyes seemed to penetrate right into him, trying to see what was going on inside. Maybe it was just bad lighting.

"Finding time to play helps balance the workload, Doctor."

"It certainly does. For other people." But it was one thing he hadn't been able to do. All playfulness and joy had seeped into the ground with his brother's blood the night that he had died. Part of Miguel had died that night, too. He hadn't been able to prevent Emilio from dying. His brother had lost his life, so what right *did he* have to one? Since that night he'd dedicated himself to serving others, saving others and sacrificing himself in the process. The clinic had become his family now, its patients his children. When one of them died, he experienced a small death, as well. Each loss was one he took personally. Each loss was one patient he'd never get back and meant the kind of endless suffering of a family that he knew all too well.

Looking at Vicky, he realized she was very observant and a little too insightful for his tastes at the moment. He'd do well to watch where those blue eyes roamed. A long time ago he might have been susceptible to their allure, but not now. For the sake of his career and community, his focus had to stay right where it was. No distractions allowed. Not even one as tempting as Victoria Sterling-Thorne. Not that he had any business associating with someone from her walk of life anyway. Worlds apart, though they lived only miles apart.

"My brother owns his own business, so I know a little

about it. All work and no play usually makes people very unhappy."

He thought of his family and the Sunday dinners, baptisms, weddings and other gatherings that he missed on a regular basis. He had been close to his family, but the kind of work he had dedicated himself to came at a price. Unfortunately, his family paid it for him. He had so much to make up for, he knew he'd never live long enough to make things right with them. His family had never blamed him for Emilio's death, though it might have been easier on him if they had. Pushing back those thoughts, he escorted her to the door. "It works this way for me." He didn't want to admit aloud that it might not be the complete truth.

"You've hired me full-time, but how many hours do you put in per week?"

"I don't keep track." If he did, he'd have to take a long, hard look at what he was doing with his life, and he didn't want to go there. This was all he deserved. It was his fault that Emilio had died. End of story. Turning away from her momentarily, he hung his lab coat on the back of a door. "Ready?"

"Thanks." She proceeded out the door ahead of him. As she walked past, he caught a whiff of her perfume, a sweet but spicy mix, not too heavy, and very enticing. It reminded him of sandalwood and musk. Through the course of the day he'd been close enough to catch it, but now it seemed to be hooked deeply into his brain. He'd know that sweet and exotic scent anywhere now.

"I'm sorry if I offended you, Dr. Torres," she said, and shoved her hands into her pockets. As she spoke, she kept her eyes averted from him. "It wasn't my intention."

"It's Miguel, and you can't offend me." He'd been through so much over the years that life had hardened him to insult or injury with mere words, and he had the scars to prove it. Offend him? Not a chance.

Her head snapped up, and she looked closely at him, peering into his eyes as if looking for something that simply wasn't there. "I find that hard to believe. We all react to things. Things can hurt us if we let them."

"Then it's simple. I don't let them." He'd walk her to her car, ensure that she got safely away and go home. Discussions of emotions weren't on the agenda for this evening.

She let that comment go, but he could see that she didn't like the answer or believe it.

In silence they walked to her car at the far end of the parking lot, and she gasped. "Oh. There's a dent in the door." She leaned over to examine it and unknowingly gave him a lovely view of her equally lovely backside.

As a professional, he knew he should avert his eyes and focus on the car door, but some deep-seated male instinct allowed him one last wistful glance before he stooped beside her to examine the damage. He pressed his fingers to the dent. It looked as if someone had opened a door onto hers and caused the dent. "Cars aren't made the way they used to be. Sometimes the wind can take a door and throw it pretty hard." He looked over at her. "Sorry about that. Maybe the parking garage down the street would be a better option." Though her car wasn't a showpiece, it was new and it showed.

"Nice idea, but it hardly does any good now."

The frown between her eyes made him want to do something to fix the situation. He was a doctor and a man and that was what he did. He fixed things. Running his fingers over the dent again, an idea surfaced. "Stay here for a minute. I'll be right back."

"Why? Do you have a dent-fixing kit in the clinic?"

"No, but I might be able to help." Despite his misgivings about Vicky, he couldn't not help her. It just wasn't in him to walk away from any situation that he could possibly fix, no matter what his personal feelings.

"I'll still have to take it to the shop, won't I?" she asked, worry clouding her eyes.

"Give me a minute, okay?" In just a few minutes he strolled across the parking lot back to Vicky and her pricey dent.

"What are you going to do?"

He swung the plunger off his shoulder to show her. "I'm going to apply a little physics to see if it will reverse your situation."

"With a plunger?" The expression on her face was full of understandable doubt. She raised her brows and stepped back. "I've got to see this."

"You'll learn to get creative if you work around here long enough." Turning to the car, he placed the plunger in the center of the dent and secured a good seal. Then he slowly pulled. The dent popped back into place with a thud, and Vicky jumped at the sound.

"You did it!" she said, and in her excitement clutched his arm with her hand. "I can't believe you did it with a *plunger,* of all things. I *never* would have thought of that."

A grin he couldn't suppress surged across his face at her contagious enthusiasm. He didn't know plumbing supplies could so easily please someone. The warmth in his chest was a puzzling sensation, one he hadn't felt for a long time. And one he couldn't afford to feel now. Stowing the pleasure at her reaction in a compartment deep inside, he nodded. "Well, there you go. Newton's third law in action."

"Equal and opposite forces, right?" She was nearly giddy in her excitement.

In the dim twilight he could see her sparkling eyes, and his gaze dropped to her mouth. It was curved upward, and her full, sensual lips were made for a man to kiss, to lose himself in, and forget the troubles of the day. Some part of him yearned to respond to that, but he couldn't. Not now. Probably not ever, and he pushed away the desire to do so. He needed her as a nurse, not a lover. This was strictly a hands-off relationship, so he changed the subject and gave his libido a kick in the shins.

"You obviously paid attention in physics."

"A little, but it's really not my forte." She gave a quick laugh then released his arm, and he could draw a full breath again. "Thanks so much, Miguel. This saves me a trip to the shop. I always feel so stupid when I go there."

"You're welcome. And you should never feel stupid. You're bright." Very—and he'd do well to remember that.

"Thanks." She dropped her chin and looked away. "My family doesn't particularly think so."

"I'd say that's their problem, then, not yours." He took a safe step back from her, removed the plunger from the door, then opened it for her. "Still willing to tackle this job?"

"Absolutely."

“Then I’ll see you in the morning.”

Before she got in, she glanced around. “I just noticed that there’s no other vehicle around. Where’s yours? Dent-free in the garage?”

“I usually walk. Burns off the day for me.” And the ghosts that haunted him every waking moment. No walk would be long enough to outdistance them.

“Do you want a lift?” she asked, and got into the vehicle. “Be happy to.”

“No, thanks. The air will do me good.” He closed the door and watched as the most intriguing woman he’d met in a very long time waved then drove away. Intriguing, yes. Within the scope of attainment? Not even on a good day. Eventually, the princess in her would come out, and then he’d see the real Vicky.

As he returned to the clinic, the mural painted on the side caught his attention. Local kids had covered the building with their art, their words and their love. It soothed his soul a little to see it. Life moved on around you, even if you were stuck in the past. Unfortunately, love wasn’t going to be enough. He’d learned that the hard way long ago. No matter how much you loved someone, it simply wasn’t enough. Life got in the way as it had when Emilio had been killed and his fiancée had left him. His own life had been on the fast track with medical school and a fiancée with golden plans for the future. That night, he’d nearly lost everything. Turning away from the sight of the building, he continued inside and stowed the plunger where it belonged.

He finished the remaining notes as quickly as possible, intending to go home and get ready for another day. As he strolled down the sidewalk, taking in the early-evening air and admiring the drawn-out sunset, thoughts of Vicky and, as much as he resented it, her words followed him home.

What was it about her that churned up the past that he'd thought had been tucked away? Maybe she reminded him of something, or of dreams let go, of an unrealized future. He didn't know and didn't want to spend another second thinking about the princess in his clinic. One day she'd walk off like everyone else had and he'd be stuck trying to replace her.

Normally, he would have walked past the photos on his wall without stopping, not allowing the memories to make him stop. Tonight he paused and really looked at the faces there as he hadn't in a long time. He paused longest in front of Emilio, who had been seventeen at the time of this photo, and he had never grown any older. In an unconscious movement he clasped the sterling-silver bracelet on his right wrist. Every time he touched it he thought of Emilio and he touched it often, scratching the surface of the memory that he could never allow to heal.

Miguel turned away from the image. He didn't need a photo. Emilio's face would be forever etched in his mind. The old cliché was that time healed all wounds. Not for him it hadn't. He couldn't let it. He didn't deserve it.

He moved away and tried to find the usual pace of his evening, but it eluded him. Images and thoughts of Emilio plagued him. Staggering guilt filled his chest and burned a path straight through his heart. The boy never should have been there, never should have come looking for him, but he had, and it *was his* fault that Emilio had died.

He'd never forgive himself for allowing his brother

to die. If only he'd been more skilled, or further in his career with enough skills, or better at convincing Emilio to leave the gang that was not a true family to him, that he had one of his own that loved him. If only he'd been a better brother, doctor, friend, Emilio would be alive right now and both their lives would be very different.

There was no fix, no absolution for that one unforgivable act. The mistake he couldn't take back and could never mend. Broken limbs he could fix. Broken lives were out of his realm. If he had minded his own business, Emilio might still be alive.

Determined not to give the entire night to the ghosts, he turned on the news, got on his stationary bike and pulled out a medical journal. One of the three were bound to distract him for a while.

CHAPTER FOUR

THE next morning Miguel strode through the front doors of the clinic, which were already unlocked, and past a waiting room full of patients. Dammit. He was late. After a restless night filled with unwanted and haunting dreams, he'd finally fallen into a deep sleep just before dawn and had apparently slept right through his alarm.

He strode to the nurses' station and shoved his hair back from his face. "Sorry, Tilly. Who do we have up first?" Trying to calm his irritation, he didn't want to be rattled when seeing patients. He could miss potential signs of illness if he were distracted. He couldn't allow himself even that small lapse. Someone's health, or life, could depend on it.

"First three rooms are full, Carlos is checking vitals and Vicky is triaging the next few," Tilly said, and glanced over her shoulder at him. "Relax, *mijo.* She's good and the world hasn't ended because you were five minutes late."

"Okay." Miguel let out a relieved breath. "Thanks, Tilly. You're a gem."

She cackled and returned to the computer screen. "More like a diamond stuck in the rough."

Still a little rattled, Miguel tended to his first two patients, with Carlos assisting. The third patient was going to require some labs and a chest X-ray that they couldn't do in the clinic. He'd have Vicky fill out the proper forms and send him to the lab and then radiology department.

The second he stepped out from the lengthy patient exam in room three, his mouth began to water, and he stopped in the doorway.

"You okay, Doc?" Carlos asked.

Miguel's gaze darted around the area. "What do I smell?"

With a chuckle Carlos clapped Miguel on the arm then pulled him out of the doorway so the patient could leave. "That would be coffee, my friend." Carlos pulled in a deep breath and sighed as if sniffing ambrosia.

"I know it's coffee. Why is it here, and why does it smell like that?" he asked, still stunned at the fragrance and his visceral reaction to it.

"Thanks to our new BFF, Vicky, we now have coffee for everyone. Really good coffee, too!" He laughed and led the way to a shiny new machine that emitted the most divine odor he'd ever smelled in this clinic.

Vicky stood beside three cases of prepackaged coffee. "I hope it's okay here. This way both the staff and patients can help themselves." Obviously pleased with the arrangement, the smile she gave was radiant.

Unfortunately, Miguel was about to wipe the smile right off of her face. "You have to send it back. I'm sorry, but I believe we talked yesterday about the budget shortfalls. We simply can't afford the luxury." He cleared his throat. "No matter what you're used to, around here money is tight and there are no unilateral decisions made."

As they spoke, an elderly patient walked by with a cup of the steaming brew in his hand. "Thanks for the coffee, miss. I sure needed a cup today." He continued on his way, oblivious to the conversation around him.

"But—"

"I'm sorry, Vicky. We can't have it."

"But—" she tried again.

"No. We can't do without medical supplies for the luxury of coffee."

Now Vicky's smile turned into an angry stare. "Your next three patients are in rooms four through six." She picked up her clipboard and entered the triage area again.

"You should listen to her, man. It's not what you think. She did a good thing for everyone." Carlos moved forward to assist a woman juggling her purse and a walker. "Let me help you with that," Carlos said to the woman, but kept his eyes on Miguel. He jerked his head in Vicky's direction and frowned at Miguel.

With a sigh, he waited until Vicky returned from the triage area. She avoided eye contact with him and walked briskly past. Damn. Late for work and now he'd offended his brand-new nurse. Could the day get any worse? "Vicky? Can I see you for a moment?" He led the way to the staff lounge and waited until she entered behind him then shut the door.

"What is it, Doctor? I have patients to see," she said, the fire still in her eyes.

"Despite my misgivings, Carlos tells me there's more to the coffee story than I know." He hated even starting this conversation, but the day was already shot to hell.

One more delay wasn't going to make it any worse. Carlos had never led him astray. Yet.

"Yes, there is." She folded her arms across her chest and stared at him.

She wasn't going to make this easy on him, and he supposed he deserved her irritation for not listening to her in the first place. In his experience, his worst-case scenario was usually right. "Will you please tell me?"

"It's simple. Happy patients come back, and they tell their friends about the place that made them happy. A little gesture like *free coffee* goes a long way in public relations. You can't put a value on word-of-mouth advertising. It's priceless. You may not think much of me, but I know that to be a fact."

"I know all of that, but—"

"So I called a friend of mine that I went to high school with. He owns a coffee delivery service."

"But—"

"And I talked him into making a *charitable donation* to the clinic for the tax write-off. *He* was pleased with my suggestion." She turned away and reached for the door.

In a split second, before he could even think about what he was doing, Miguel reached over her head and slammed the door shut, trapping her between the door and his body.

With a gasp she whirled and raised her face to his, only inches away. "Open this door."

"No. Not until you listen to me."

"You didn't listen to me. Why should I listen to you now?" She continued to glare up at him, and he could see every speck, every detail of the irises of her eyes, and the way the pupils changed.

"I'm not letting you out of here until you let me apologize." Though it nearly choked him to say it, it was the right thing to do.

Surprise covered her face for an unguarded second, and her pupils dilated at the rush of pleasure his words caused. When her lips parted, they drew his attention. If he were a different man in a different situation, he wouldn't have hesitated to close the gap between them and find out how soft her lips were. If he were a different man, he'd take her in his arms and press her length against his. But he wasn't, and he didn't. He couldn't.

When she blinked and looked at him with a softening in her expression that made him want more than anything to take that step, he choked down that feeling of want that she unknowingly stirred in him. The muscles in his arms trembled from the effort of holding himself back. Sweat beaded on his forehead and he began to lean forward, began to make that move toward her. Something in him held back and he froze.

They remained locked in that position for a few more seconds until Miguel slid his hand down the door to the knob. If he didn't hold on to something he was going to make a move he'd likely regret.

"I'm sorry, Vicky. I should have listened to you before I jumped to conclusions. I was irritated at being late and starting out the day so far behind in patients. It won't happen again, I promise." He took a step back from her and drew in a deep breath, shaken by the memories that statement roused. "I overslept this morning, which always puts me in a foul mood."

"I accept your apology, but the coffee situation is totally your fault."

"What?" Now that certainly got his attention. "How?"

"After you fixed my car with the plunger, you said that when working around here you had to be creative." She let out a small laugh and the tension visibly left her shoulders. "After that awful coffee you made me yesterday, I decided to get creative with that first." A shrug lifted her shoulders. "Didn't hurt to ask my friend, you know?"

A grin split Miguel's face and he relaxed, too. "Okay. I'll take responsibility for that."

A light rap on the door made them both jump, as if they had been guilty of doing something other than talking.

"We've got patients out here," Carlos said through the door.

"Oh, dear." Vicky pulled the door open and nearly collided with the assistant. "Sorry, Carlos. We had to get something straightened out."

"Yeah. And thanks for the coffee," he said. "Everybody loves it."

"That's great."

"Think you could do something about doughnuts next?" The young man grinned and raced off to collect the next patient.

Vicky laughed. "He's a great kid, isn't he?" she asked Miguel as they left the lounge.

"He is. I hope he stays."

"Why wouldn't he stay?"

"He's got bigger dreams than this clinic. At this point he thinks he wants to be a doctor. He's got a long road ahead, if he really pursues it." Miguel sighed, having already walked the path that Carlos wanted to take.

"You did it, why couldn't Carlos?" she asked. "Seriously. There's the state-funded lottery program he could apply for. As long as he graduated from high school, it's guaranteed for college, right?"

"Yes. I just hope he doesn't get...distracted." The way his brother had, which had led to his demise.

"Well, guess we need to get back to the patients for now, and work on Carlos's future later, right?"

"Yes." He was pleased that they had solved the issue so quickly and so well and were right back to their professional roles. Contacting a coffee service for a donation wasn't something that would have occurred to him. Maybe someone who came from a different background could be beneficial to the clinic. Time would tell.

"Why don't you try the coffee?" she asked, and poured him a cup which he accepted, his fingers brushing over hers.

"I'm afraid my taste buds might keel over from exposure to real flavor," he said, but took a sip anyway. He groaned in reluctant delight. "Be sure to thank your friend for me. This is fabulous."

Vicky flushed with pleasure at his reaction. No man in her life had ever been as satisfied with something as simple as a cup of coffee. "I will." She dashed off into a patient room.

CHAPTER FIVE

ONLY after Vicky got home that evening did she allow herself to relive the moments when Miguel had trapped her in the lounge. She'd been horribly angry at him. At first it had seemed that he was treating her exactly the same way her father and brothers did, as if she didn't have a brain in her head. The same way her ex-husband had treated her. But then Miguel had changed and listened to her. He had been so close, so masculine, so very attractive and totally off-limits. He'd said it would never happen again. That's what had dissolved her anger. She wanted to believe him, but trust came so hard to her. After the life-changing experience with her former husband, trust was not something she handed out like candies. She'd put her trust and faith in a man, supposedly for the remainder of her life, and with that weapon he'd turned her world upside down.

Closing her eyes, she allowed her mind to take the image further than it had gone in the lounge. If she had raised her face just right, if he had reached out just so, it would only have taken an inch or two before their lips had met. Vicky melted into the dream for a second, wondering just what a kiss with Dr. Torres would be like.

The phone rang and she jumped, and the fantasy spiraled away. Before picking up the phone, she checked the caller ID. It was her brother, Edward.

"Hey, Eddy."

"You're the only one in the world that calls me that, you know."

She heard the affectionate irritation in his voice, and she smiled. "That's 'cos I'm your little sister. You'll always be Eddy to me, no matter how successful you are as a big-shot designer."

"Just, please, don't call me that around anyone in the business. I'd never live it down."

"Hey, I just had an idea. You could create a whole new line of clothing for kids called Eddy Wear, or something like that." How strange. That idea had never occurred to her before and a little bubble of pleasure rippled through her. Then she bit her lip, waiting for his response. He'd never taken suggestions from her before, so why would he now?

He chuckled. "That's funny, Victoria." He chuckled again. "Really funny, but I'll have to think about that one, if you don't mind."

She mentally sighed, knowing that she would always be the little sister with ideas that never went anywhere to him. "So, what's up? Why are you calling? I know it wasn't to get fashion advice."

"You are *so* right. I was wondering if you'd like to come to a little dinner engagement with me."

Another sigh escaped her. He always called on her when he needed a date. He was married to his design business, jetting off for meetings and shows in New York and Europe, so dating was a chore for him. "What, when, where and all that stuff?"

Edward gave her the details, and she checked her calendar. Two weeks' time on a Friday night. She certainly didn't have a date either. "Sure."

"Great! I'll send a few new designs for you to choose from, and the limo will pick you up at six-thirty." Always one to take advantage of publicity opportunities, Eddy insisted that she wear his designs at these outings of his and anytime they were at an event together. Fortunately, nothing was indecent or had too many frills, and always complimented her figure, so how could she argue with that?

"Will Daddy be there?" She hated asking that, but it was better for her to be prepared with her Victoria face on when he was near. That mantle she wore helped to protect her emotions from the pain that usually ensued. When she was unprepared, he always seemed to hurt her with his judgments and opinions of her life. Being on guard and prepared around him took the sting out of some of his comments.

"No, Charles was invited but has another engagement." For whatever reason, Eddy always called their father by his given name. "Secretly, I think he's seeing someone and doesn't want us to know about it," Eddy said in a dramatic whisper.

"Why not, for heaven's sake? We're adults, and Mother died a very long time ago." Perhaps if he had a romantic diversion, he'd take things easier on her. Running her life seemed to be a hobby for him, and he definitely could use some distraction.

"I think that he thinks that *we* think he's being disloyal to her memory by getting involved with someone, and you know how he is about loyalty."

Vicky could imagine the eye-roll that Eddy put on

just then, and she laughed. "I do indeed." It was part of the reason they had fought so much when she had declared her major in college. She wanted to leave the family business behind for a hands-on career. It was the only battle she'd ever won with her father, but he'd by no means forgotten about it. He was so much prouder of his two sons than of his daughter, whom he viewed as a failure. Failed marriage, failed career, failed daughter.

"Well, I've got to go, Eddy. I'll see you at the event."

"See you there, baby sister. Can't wait for you to see the gowns I'm sending."

After hanging up the phone, she poured a glass of wine to settle the sudden nerves in her stomach. A simple Chablis, but it was her favorite wine from the family vineyard. New Mexico was the oldest wine-growing region in America, thanks to the Spanish settlers of long ago. Although her family was not of Spanish descent, they had purchased stock from the original vines and developed their own holdings, which had been in the family ever since. That was the loyalty that Eddy had been talking about. It ran as deep in her family as the vines in the ground.

The vineyard grew on acreage that had once been the bottom of a very large, very ancient ocean. The land left behind after the ocean had receded millions of years ago was some of the most fertile in the country. This location so close to the Rio Grande River provided the only thing lacking when Mother Nature didn't cooperate: fresh water.

Looking out the picture window of her little caretaker cottage, she enjoyed the lavish view of row upon row of grapes. As a child she'd raced and hidden among the lush canopy of leaves and vines, using her imagination to create stories that had taken her to exotic and wondrous lands where she had been queen.

Now the vineyards were waking up after being dormant all winter. New Mexico springs usually began in April and the growing season stretched out to the first frost, sometimes as late as October. This was her favorite time of year, when the earth renewed itself and grew to face another season of glorious bounty.

The cottage was her sanctuary. After her divorce she'd needed to be in the middle of the vineyard where nature soothed her, not in the bustle of the main house where every move she made was scrutinized and watched. There she could never truly relax and just be herself. This cottage was where she'd needed to be. It had provided the protection and safety she'd needed, and demanded nothing of her. If she had her choice, she'd never leave its secure walls unless she found something its equal.

Now, wine in hand, she opened her door and took an evening stroll through the vines, enjoying visualizing the journey of the grapes and drinking the end results. Life came full circle right there in front of her. Touching a leaf or vine here and there, she wondered if she could remember some of those stories she'd told herself as a child. It would be good to be queen again, if only for a while.

Miguel sighed as he looked at the prospectus in front of him. He'd had some mad idea about presenting it to potential private investors like their previous benefactor, but it was hopeless. The clinic lost money every year thanks to the economy, higher health costs and lack of reimbursement. No sane investor was going to put money on this dark horse. After a quick glance at the clock, he saved the file then closed the computer document. He'd fiddle with it some more later. Right now he had to get to the community center or he was going to be late for his standing Wednesday night basketball game. After a quick change from his scrubs into ratty exercise attire and filling a water bottle, he headed out.

In a few minutes he reached the community center that had saved his life more than once over the years. He and some of his cousins had practically grown up here, and he had a special affection for this building and the people who ran it. Blood and roots ran deep in the south valley of Albuquerque.

"M., you ready for a whooping?" his cousin Arturo asked, and tossed a ball to him. Miguel caught it and automatically began to dribble it, the thump of the ball on the floor corresponding with his heartbeat.

"After last week I don't think you have it in you." He grinned and tossed the ball back.

Arturo caught it, then made a quick spin and charged the net, catching Miguel off guard. "How's that?"

"Got me on that one," Miguel said with a grin, and the game began in earnest. They played and carried on for an hour before either one was willing to be the first to take a water break. Hot and sweaty and thoroughly drained, Miguel parked himself against the wall and caught his breath. Although they were cousins, he and Arturo were friends, too. Each knew the other's deep, dark secrets and was willing to keep them that way.

"Are you coming to the graduation party?" Arturo asked.

"What graduation party?" he asked, and frowned. Arturo didn't have any kids graduating.

"Don't you check your email? I sent it to you a couple of weeks ago. Cindy is graduating high school."

"Cindy?" Miguel cringed. "No way. Did I miss something? She's only a junior, right? She should have another year."

"You're behind the times, dude. She's been in an accelerated program all year, taking high school and beginning college classes at the same time. She's finishing a year early so we're having a big celebration."

"How did she get so smart?" No one in their family had been accelerated like that.

"Takes after her mother's side of the family," Arturo said, and drank some more water. "So how's the clinic? Still making a good wife?"

"What?"

"You're married to that clinic of yours. You don't date, you don't go out to meet anyone, all you do is work." He drained the contents of his water bottle. "You are turning into an old man way too soon, my friend."

Miguel turned suspicious eyes on Arturo. "Now you sound like my mother. Have you been talking to her?" That wouldn't surprise him. She'd been trying to match him up with someone, anyone, for years.

"Oh, no, not really." Arturo looked away, then back at Miguel, and shrugged. "She talked to my mother, who talked to me."

A laugh creaked out of Miguel as his suspicions were confirmed. "I knew she was in there somewhere. What's she up to now?"

"She worries. They both do. You need to get out a

little more, M. She's afraid you're becoming an old man way before your time."

"No worries. I'll be fine." The concern in Arturo's face puzzled him. Didn't they know he could take care of himself, that he always had, and didn't depend on anyone? But later Miguel wondered if their fears were coming true. Was he turning into an old man while still in his early thirties? After his fiancée had left him years ago, he'd never really tried to get out there into the dating arena much. Too busy, too intense, too many things to do that didn't include leisure time spent on relationships. Oh, once in a while he'd hook up for a mutually temporary situation, but those were few and far between. His thoughts turned to Vicky and he wondered if she had any better luck at relationships than he did. With her looks and background she likely had men lined up for her. But, then, that could pose its own set of problems.

He showered, changed, ate something, all the while wondering about Arturo's seemingly innocent statement. Was he right? Maybe that's why it wouldn't leave his mind and continued to nag him like an imminent case of flu coming on.

When *was* the last time he'd had a date or even gone out for coffee with a woman that wasn't business related? He couldn't remember. Last year? Maybe the year before? Miguel blew out a long sigh. Arturo could be right. He *was* married to his work and hadn't even realized it. Based on principle alone, he was going to have to do something about it.

The next day passed smoothly, and the coffee service continued to be a huge success with staff as well as patients. Pastries magically appeared and Carlos was ecstatic.

Arturo's words followed Miguel around like a shadow. If he turned quickly enough, he thought he might actually see them lurking behind him, goading him on.

He and Vicky continued to work efficiently together. At least that part of his life was going well. Until he had to close the clinic forever. He was beginning to think that Vicky's idea of a major fundraiser would be the only way to save it. But that was a topic for another day. First things first.

The afternoon wound down and the last patient had been seen. The familiar pattern, the flow of the day, had soothed him at one time. He could trust in the continuity of his work, but today it didn't seem to be working.

"You okay, Miguel?" Vicky asked, perceptive as ever. "You seem a bit off today."

"I'm good. Just got something on my mind."

She leaned against the desk and put her purse down. "I've got time to talk if you want to." She shrugged and her glance skittered away. "I mean, if you'd like to. It helps sometimes."

Miguel thought a second. Maybe she could help. Mirroring her position, he moved and leaned against the desk beside her. "Well, I have a problem. A woman problem."

"Oh," she said. "I didn't know you were involved with anyone." Her shoulders sagged a little. "Not that it's any of my business, but how can I help?"

A grin split his face at her reaction, though it shouldn't have pleased him. "It's a female *cousin* problem."

Vicky brightened and met his gaze. "What kind of problem is that?"

"She's graduating this weekend from high school. I need to figure out what kind of present to get her for her party on Saturday."

"Cash. It always works for kids that age." She shook her head. "My oldest brother has three kids, and that's what they always want. Cash, cash, cash. And you're off the hook from having to think too hard about it. A card, a check, they can buy whatever they want, and you don't have to feel bad if they didn't like what you got." She snapped her fingers. "Done."

Miguel narrowed his gaze on her. "I like the way you think." That would be the simplest solution and he was chagrined that he hadn't thought of it himself. Arturo was looking more right all the time.

"I was a teenage girl once. I have the inside scoop."

For a few seconds their gazes locked, and Miguel thought about her as a teenager. "I'll bet you were pestered by all the boys in school, weren't you?"

A quick laugh chirped out of her. "Hardly. I was awkward, too tall, too skinny, introverted and...well, my mother died when I was sixteen, so that made life more difficult than it could have been, I guess."

The momentary flirtation in his gut evaporated at her words. "I didn't mean to pry, Vicky. I'm sorry."

"You're not prying and it's fine. It's been over ten years, so for the most part I've put it to rest."

He gave a mental sigh, feeling a connection to her that surprised him. "I also lost someone when I was young. My brother." He hadn't meant to tell her about Emilio, but the words just popped out.

"I'm so sorry. It's tough, isn't it?" she asked, offering unexpected sympathy. "I think sometimes it makes us better caregivers because we know what it's like to lose someone. Just wish that it had been different, you know?"

"Yeah, believe me, I know." Sadness crept into her eyes and something cramped in Miguel's chest. He knew that feeling exactly and he didn't want to share it with anyone, let alone Vicky. They were poles apart in so many ways. Finding common ground between them was impossible. At least, that's what he'd thought. Pain shared with another often took the sting out of it, but he couldn't imagine that happening with her.

"So, is your cousin having a big bash or just running off with her presents?"

The change of topic was a welcome one, and he returned to the present situation. "It's a big deal—family, an outdoor tent, the whole thing."

"Judging by your reaction, not one you're eager to attend?"

He frowned and crossed his arms over his chest. "It's not that I'm unhappy about it, it's good to be with family and all that."

"I sense a *but* coming."

A long-suffering sigh rolled out of him and he tried not to groan. "At these types of events, I get just hounded about being single. *Are you dating anyone, are you going to ever get married?* All that stuff. I'm sure it's not something you suffer at your own family events. Your family experience may be quite different than mine."

A snort was her only answer.

He shook his head then something occurred to him. If he took a date, everyone would back off and give him a breather. It had potential. Now, who could he get to go with him who wouldn't read anything into it?

"I suppose you're the only single man there, too."

"No. Just the grandson who hasn't fulfilled his family and reproductive obligations." He turned slightly toward her. "So, uh, what are you doing for the weekend?" Was he mad for even thinking of asking her to help him out? People like her didn't help people like him, but desperation pumped through him, and he was willing to risk nearly anything to get out of this.

"No plans, really. I'm just going to be in and out, errands and that kind of stuff." Then her gaze flashed to his and shock widened her eyes as she realized what he was up to. "Are you serious?"

"Dead serious. I need you to protect me."

She almost snorted out a laugh. "How am I going to protect you?"

"Well, at least people will think twice about grilling me about my future reproductive plans if I have a date on my arm."

"You're really serious?" The smile faded away. "Are you certain that I'm the right person for the job? Doesn't Carlos have sisters you can borrow or anything?"

"He does, but my family knows them, so they'd know it's a sham. You're the only one who can help me out." As much as he hated to admit it, she was the best person for the job. His family didn't know her and she wouldn't give him any unrealistic expectations about their relationship. Strictly business. "How about you wear a nice summer dress, bring your appetite, and pretend to be my date for an afternoon?" Asking her out was another thing he hadn't planned on doing, but now that it was out there between them, his heart sped up and his stomach clenched, waiting for her reply. Her gaze held his for a few seconds longer, considering, and he could almost hear her debating the issue mentally.

"Okay, I'll be your date and spare you from your family for an afternoon. But you're going to owe me one, buster."

"Totally. You have no idea how much I appreciate this."

She sighed. "I'm beginning to feel I'm forever the bridesmaid, never the bride. My brother always hits me up for functions, too."

They made arrangements to meet at the office and Miguel would drive from there. "See you tomorrow."

CHAPTER SIX

WELL, that hadn't been the kind of ending to her day that she'd expected. Who said miracles didn't happen anymore? Miguel had asked her out. Sort of. It wasn't really a date, but a pretend date, so she shouldn't get too excited about it. That wasn't something she'd ever have expected, especially after the rocky start to her job.

All the same, little flutters stirred in her stomach. The man was gorgeous and single. How much better could a day get than spending an afternoon with him, whether it was a real date or not? She'd never been to a graduation party as he'd described. Those sorts of functions in her family tended to be held at the country club, not the backyard at her cousin's house. The decorating and cleanup could be left to the staff, but then you missed the fun of it. Should be an enjoyable way to spend an afternoon, especially as she didn't have anything else do to and it was an opportunity to stay away from the homestead and her father's oppressive energy. Over the years she'd learned just to avoid him rather than engaging in endless arguments that she'd never win anyway. One day she hoped to mend her relationship with her father, but until he was open to it, it would never happen.

Miguel was so different from the men in her family.

He put himself out there for others, and she couldn't imagine her father extending himself in the same way. Her ex-husband had been a carbon copy of her father and just as cold. A man who'd taken his money to bed instead of his wife. As a result their marriage had ended within months. Back then she'd deluded herself into thinking that the intimacy she craved in a relationship was something she could live without, that there were other things she could be happy with. She'd been so wrong about that and about the man she'd married. Her judgment in men had always been poor, but it had been totally missing when she'd agreed to marry Carl. In the end, she'd chosen to correct the mistake before bringing children into the picture. She and Carl had parted ways, with him happily counting the settlement money that had been more important than she had been. That had been the end of any romantic endeavors in the past few years. Sticking to being her brother's date now and then had gotten her out of the house but kept her safe enough from any awkward entanglements. Tomorrow was only one day out of her life, and she was doing a favor for her boss. That was simple, wasn't it?

That night Vicky slept with dreams disturbing the peace of the night. Dreams of unfulfilled longings stirred her body to a blistering heat that woke her. Images of Miguel, his face tantalizingly close to hers, teased her through the night. If only she had reached out to him the other day, her night might not be so restless. Until the early hour before dawn she slept fitfully, trying to ignore the call of her body, the yearning to hold another close.

Years had passed since she'd been intimate with anyone. Getting hot over her coworker was just a case of familiarity and having an attractive man right in front of her every day, right?

Her dreams and her subconscious knew otherwise.

As they drove to the party, Miguel ran through the extensive list of relatives she was most likely to encounter.

"You know I'll never remember all that," she said, and gave him a smile that looked more like a grimace. She didn't want to disappoint him, but she was afraid she was going to. And she had to keep reminding herself that this wasn't a date but a favor, so the same rules didn't apply. The little butterfly careening around in her stomach wasn't convinced.

"I know, I know. I have a huge family. If we stick close, I can refresh you as we go along. You'll be fine."

"I hope you know what you're doing, Miguel."

After a quick glance, he said, "I do, too." Then he patted her hand. "It'll be fine. No matter what happens. It's just one day, right? Then we go back to our lives and call it good."

Before Vicky could even think of what to say, Miguel pulled his truck up against the curb and parked behind a line of other vehicles. "We'll have to walk from here, but it's just a block or two."

In minutes they had arrived at a very large outdoor tent filled with people of all ages. She turned to stare at Miguel. "This isn't a party, this is an event. You could fill Isotopes Park with this many people."

"Now, that's a slight exaggeration, but I told you there would be a mob of people here. Let's find the food. I'm dying for my cousin's enchiladas. His green-chili stew is outstanding." He grinned and took her hand.

The feel of her trim hand in his surprised him. The surprise was that it felt immediately comfortable, not in the size of her fingers or the silky softness of her skin or even the way her fingers naturally curled against his palm. It was the fit. A fit he hadn't expected and one that he wasn't sure he should even be thinking about, even in the loosest of terms. Guilt surfaced in him. Guilt that he wanted a life of his own to enjoy while leaving the memory of his brother behind. That couldn't happen. Tension knotted his shoulders, but he tried not to show it.

Today was all about getting him out of a jam, and Vicky was nice enough to help him out. That was all. He knew that there would never be any chance at things going beyond today because he wouldn't allow it.

Somehow they made it through the mob of people and to the food line. It just seemed natural to have Vicky in front of him and for him to place his hands on her shoulders, and he tried very hard not to feel the silky softness of her skin bared enticingly by the thin straps of her summer dress. The sun shone down on the day and it was a gorgeous afternoon. Miguel started to relax as he introduced Vicky to some of his family. When he got to his mother, he hugged her tight, then took Vicky's hand and introduced them.

"It's been so long since my son has brought a woman to meet the family." The woman with intelligent brown eyes, the same chocolate shade as Miguel's, took her hand from him. "It is good to see him socializing, but I can see why he's kept you to himself." She started to lead Vicky away from Miguel.

The panicked look Vicky cast over her shoulder at him nearly broke his resolve. There was desperation in those eyes, which he worked hard to resist. Something, some protective male instinct he'd nearly forgotten about, surfaced strong and fast in him. Before he knew it he'd stepped forward without taking his eyes from Vicky. As much as he'd tried to ignore it, push it away or flat out deny it, there was something going on between them. Some attraction that he hadn't felt in years. Although it wasn't exactly welcome, he couldn't stop it. Walking away from that was going to be difficult, no matter what his head told him. His heart and the heat in his blood told him something entirely different. Aside from that, he couldn't let his mother take over or she'd find out their whole ruse in seconds. "We were going to eat first then catch up with everyone."

"See that you do, *mijo,* see that you do." She patted his cheek as her perceptive eyes watched him. "I've missed seeing you with the family."

He took Vicky's hand in his and led her to a row of chairs where they balanced their plates on their knees.

"This is quite the party, isn't it?" she asked, breaking the silence between them. She tucked her hair behind her ear, not wanting to let Miguel know that she'd never been to a party like this but that she was totally prepared to enjoy herself. The nerves she had now weren't at all like the nerves she had when she was at a society event. Now it was all because of Miguel's presence so close to her.

"Yes, it is. Cindy's the oldest of my cousin Arturo's kids and is a really smart girl. She's graduating a year early and already taking university classes." Small talk helped break the tension in the air between them. "I was never that dedicated when I was her age."

"Wow, neither was I. I was lucky to get through some

of my classes, let alone graduate early." Vicky shook her head. "Math was the bane of my existence."

"I'll take your word for that." He looked over at her as she sat with her plate on her knees. "Before anything else happens, I want to thank you for coming." If nothing else, he owed her his gratitude. He couldn't see behind her sunglasses, but he thought she winked at him. The sideways smile she gave him, with her lips just turned up, made his heart lurch. Vicky was simply gorgeous, and he wondered why she wasn't taken. If he'd been looking, he might have been looking at her. Yet there was that bloom of attraction between them that lay waiting to unfold.

"Just remember you owe me one." She laughed and shook her head, then tucked her hair behind her ear in a gesture he was beginning to realize was a nervous habit.

He laughed and suddenly felt much better, his heart lighter than it had been in years. It was a good feeling and one he didn't want to let go of just yet. It reminded him of the way he had lived a long time ago, before the death of Emilio and the ruining of his life. "I won't forget. Promise."

Arturo dropped into the seat beside Miguel. They spoke a moment in Spanish then Arturo turned to Vicky. "So, you're the new nurse, right?"

"Right."

"Has your mother met her yet?" Arturo asked with a big grin.

"Yes." Miguel nodded his head.

"She like?"

"Yes, I think so. But just so you know, Vicky's only helping me out for the day." As Miguel said the words, for a moment he wanted them not to be true. Watching Vicky sit beside him, seeing the sunlight glint off the highlights in her hair, he wanted to really have her in his life. But what could he do, fire her and then ask her out? That wasn't going to happen. The clinic was much more important than his pitiful social life. He needed her as a nurse, not a date right now, although unofficially Vicky was his date. For today.

"Yeah, right." Arturo leaned over and shook Vicky's hand. "Anyway, welcome to the party. Be sure to have a glass of wine or something before it's all gone."

"I will, thanks. By the way, your chili is fantastic—what do you do special to it? I don't do much cooking, but for this I'd learn."

"Oh, a little of this and that. I don't write anything down." He waved his hand as if waving away her request. "Have you ever seen the movie *Like Water For Chocolate?*"

"No." She'd never heard of it, but it sounded intriguing. Anything with chocolate in the title had to be good. She took a quick glance at Miguel, but he seemed to be paying close attention to his cousin. A little pang fluttered inside her. What had she been thinking, agreeing to this nondate? Was she thinking that Miguel would somehow put aside his biases, ignore the glaring chasm between their backgrounds? She refocused on Arturo. "What's it about?"

"Rent it sometime. My recipe is just like that. Passion in every ingredient."

Vicky narrowed her eyes. She was certain he was teasing her, but she wasn't really sure. "I'll do that."

"Stop teasing her, will you? You're no gourmet,

you just won't give up that recipe that you stole from Grandma."

Arturo grinned, but didn't deny the friendly accusation. "I've gotta go anyway. It's tough, being the host." He gave a casual wave and wandered off through the crowd.

After they'd finished eating, Miguel stood. "I guess there's no way around it, I'm going to have to introduce you to people."

"I'm ready." She held her hands out to him, and he pulled her to her feet. With the uneven surface of the ground, she bobbled a little bit on her sandals, and Miguel placed a hand on her hip to steady her.

"Okay?"

For a second she didn't answer, just looked at him and swallowed. "Yeah, I'm good." If they had met in a different place and time or were from more similar backgrounds, maybe then they could have been on a more equal footing. The buzz of attraction that hung in the air every time they were near each other hadn't gone unnoticed by her. She simply didn't trust in herself or her judgment in men to be able to reach out to Miguel. The fire of her past had burned away any confidence she might have once had and she still had the singe marks to prove it. The idea of reaching out to another man had her quaking inside. Because of her upbringing and the need to keep up appearances, she didn't let her fears show. God forbid that anyone should see outright emotion in a Sterling-Thorne. Not that Miguel would believe her anyway. The man was the most fearless person she'd ever seen. Nothing scared him, and he wouldn't understand her fears, so it was best to hide them beneath a bright smile. With one last glance at his tempting mouth and mysterious eyes, she released her grip on his arm and let him lead her through the crowd on their nondate. "Let's go."

As they made the rounds, it seemed perfectly natural for Miguel to place his hand on her shoulder, touch her arm, take her hand and tuck it into his elbow. Although this started out as a way for him to keep his family from asking questions, he was allowing himself to fall deeply into the role he'd set up for himself. For the next few hours he enjoyed the luxury of touching her whenever he could, and she never pulled away from his touch but rather seemed to enjoy it. Each time Vicky turned her face up to his, he wanted to bring her closer, but knew that was the wrong thing to do—for both of them.

"You have a lovely family, but I think I'm ready for some wine or a spritzer now," she said, and fanned her face with her hand. "Whew."

"Let's go. Me, too. I've had about enough talking for a while." He glanced at his watch and was surprised at how much time had passed. He was enjoying himself more than he had thought he would. Thanks to Vicky. He certainly was going to owe her a big favor. They arrived at the refreshment table, which was tucked into a corner of the yard beneath a sprawling cottonwood tree that offered the welcome shelter of shade. He looked up into the branches, which seemed different than they had been in childhood. Perspective, he guessed. All things changed with time.

"What's up?" She gave his hand a squeeze.

"Nothing, really. I was just thinking of the times I climbed this tree." He looked down at Vicky. "This was my grandmother's house first, and I spent a lot of time here as a kid. Good memories..." He only wished that some of them could have been different.

"I didn't climb trees, but I spent a lot of time in the gardens and vineyards when I was a kid, just wandering and getting away, you know?" She looked away from him, then at the beverages. "I wonder what kind of wine they have."

"Arturo likes local wines, so it's hard to tell what's here." Miguel reached for a bottle and held it up. "This one's from Gruet Winery."

Vicky leaned over his arm and read the label. "Oh, that's lovely. I know that one."

"Isn't that one of your competitors?" he asked with a sly grin.

"Yes, they are, but what's business without competition? Makes everything taste better when the batch is done, you know?"

"Are you serious? Isn't the wine business as cutthroat as any other?"

"It can be, I guess, I just prefer to stay away from that part of it and focus on the results." She paused a second and then took the glass that he held out to her, not caring what it was at this point, just grateful for it and the breather it gave her. Having Miguel so close and allowing him to touch her was something she'd not normally have done. Each touch, each time his body grazed hers sent ripples of awareness through her. "So, where's your cousin's daughter? We haven't met her yet."

"I know. She must be holding court somewhere. I'm sure we'll see her pretty soon. She's not exactly the shy-and-retiring type."

A squeal announced the arrival of the party girl, Cindy.

"Miguel!" The teenager launched herself at him. He caught her but had to take a step back from the force and the wine in his hand sloshed over the rim.

"Wow. Is this my little Cindy?" he asked, and twirled her around in a quick circle.

"It's me. All grown up now!" With a laugh she stood beside him but kept her arm around his waist as he introduced her to Vicky. "I'm so glad you came."

"Wouldn't miss it." He ignored the twinge of guilt when the little voice inside him reminded him that he almost had, that his guilt had kept him away. "Where have you been?"

A dramatic roll of her eyes was all the answer he needed. "Got to make nice with the aunties before I can play, you know?"

"I know what you mean." He reached into his shirt pocket and extracted a long, slender envelope and held it out.

Cindy snatched it from his hand with another signature squeal. "Ooh! What is it, what is it, what is it?" She tore the envelope to shreds and extracted the card containing a check. "Thank you, thank you, thank you!" She hugged him again and dashed off.

"What a bundle of energy. No wonder she's an overachiever," Vicky said with a laugh. "She adores you."

"It's mutual. Sometimes I feel bad that I haven't been around more." He looked away and then sipped his wine.

"Well, the good thing is that you're here now, right? Life gets in the way for us all." Hesitation in her move, she reached out and placed her hand on his forearm. There was strength there in the muscles covered by tawny skin, but there was steel that she sensed beneath the surface.

"I appreciate that," he said, and held her gaze for a moment. "There are a few more people I want to find then we can go."

CHAPTER SEVEN

AFTERNOON sun gave way to evening shadows. Vicky was enjoying herself immensely and felt the chains of anxiety relinquishing their hold on her. Even the chat with Miguel's mother wasn't as intimidating as she'd thought it was going to be. The woman was lovely, had raised a fine son and was very proud of his achievements. Though there was a touch of caution in her eyes when she looked at him, she obviously loved him. Emotions stirred inside her. Seeing the love of his mother reminded her of what she had lost so long ago. The grief that she'd dealt with at the loss of her mother surfaced briefly in her heart. The pang of her loss nearly brought tears to her eyes as she watched Miguel and his mother, but she choked them back, trying not to allow envy for something that could never be claim any of this day.

Just as she thought the party was going to wind down, a band began to play.

Excitement danced in Miguel's eyes and she was nearly mesmerized. "Part two—music. It's not a party without music and dancing, is it?" Miguel asked, grabbing her hand.

"I thought we were going to leave?" Panic set in. This wasn't the kind of music she knew.

"Sorry. Change in plan—do you mind?" He tugged on her hand.

"Wait! I don't know this stuff. I'm strictly ballroom. This is…I don't know what this is!" Although she protested, she was helpless to stop Miguel as he led the way to the makeshift dance floor. What if she embarrassed herself?

"That's okay. I'll lead."

And lead he did. Every move they made together was directed by Miguel. His hands spun her, led her through each step as if he were a dance instructor. Within a few minutes Vicky relaxed and just let him lead her. It was what she wanted anyway. Never in her life had she felt so feminine, so light, so enchanted by a man in the moonlight.

When the music finally slowed down, Vicky thought that Miguel was going to take her back to sit down, but he simply drew her closer to him. The tiny lights strung around the yard created interesting halos of light and deep pockets of shadowy darkness in the corners of the yard.

Miguel tucked Vicky close against him with his chin against her right temple. She felt a sigh roll through him, and she closed her eyes, letting go, letting the sensations of the day and the feel of Miguel's body be her guide. The flames that had singed her in the past gave way to a new heat source.

Each move they made together was guided by his hand in the small of her back. The man was an expert dancer, and Vicky found herself unwilling and unable to resist the desire that bubbled up inside her. What if, for once, she made a move unlike any she'd ever made? What if she reached out to Miguel? Would he hold on or would he burn her, the way every other man she'd known had burned her?

Leaning back slightly, she needed to see his face, to look into his eyes, to see if she was simply fooling herself into believing that something was going on between them. Could she have imagined the tenderness in every touch of his hand, the want in every move of his body toward her?

Now, looking up at his face, the way his eyes held her gaze then dropped to her mouth and lingered there, she knew she hadn't imagined anything. Automatically, her lips parted as Miguel guided them around to the music. Her heart raced and it wasn't from the exercise of the dancing. She wanted Miguel with everything she had in her. Shadows darkened around them as Miguel led her into a quiet sanctuary of the yard. The music faded to a dull rhythm far away as the roar of her heart crowded out all other sound.

The hand at her waist eased up her back until it cupped the back of her head. "Vicky," he whispered, and bent his head toward her. "This may be the worst move I'll ever make, but I want to kiss you."

Needing no encouragement, she raised her face and met his lips. The instant their lips touched, a shock of deep desire rolled through Vicky. She parted her lips and eagerly met his tongue with hers, melting against him and clasping his neck with her hands. He gathered her tight against his body and squeezed her, kissed her, as if ravenous for the taste and touch of her. As if she were the very thing he needed to sustain life.

No woman had ever felt this way to him. Miguel held on to her as if she were a dream, a wisp of smoke that would fly away if he didn't hold tight. This night was enchanted, and Vicky was the magic in his arms.

Heart racing, desire pulsed through him as he kissed her and held her. In less than a second he forgot where they were and lost himself in the feel of Vicky's curves against him. She was trim, but lush in all the right places. The feel of her soft breasts crushed against his chest made him wish they were somewhere else. Anywhere else.

When he finally lifted his head, his breathing was ragged, as if he'd run ten city blocks. Desire hung in the air, hot and heavy between them. They simply stared at each other as if in shock. Maybe they were. Maybe it was an enchanted evening and they were under the spell of the night.

"Wow." She brushed her hair back from her face with a hand that visibly trembled. "Wrong move or not, I certainly didn't expect that."

"Neither did I. I hope I haven't offended you?"

"Being offended never entered my mind," she said, and placed her palm on his chest over his heart. "I…feel…more alive right now than I think I've ever been." Then she looked away, as if embarrassed by her admission.

With a finger under her chin, he raised her face so that she looked at him again. "So am I," he whispered, and it was the biggest truth he'd faced in a long, long time.

Over the course of an afternoon he'd begun to fall for Vicky Sterling-Thorne.

At last they said their goodbyes and left the party. They drove back to the clinic in silence. Miguel maintained his loose hold on her hand as he drove. Pulling into the parking lot of the clinic, he stopped beside her car and didn't know what to say.

"Thanks for a lovely day." Vicky spoke first.

"I need to thank you. It was certainly more pleasant than I expected it to be."

She smiled at that. "I think there was one part that neither of us expected." Shyly, she glanced down and then curved a hand around one ear, tucking the hair back from her face.

"Definitely." That was an understatement. There was so much about today, about Vicky and himself, that he hadn't ever expected. There were things about her that were incredibly appealing, but as the bubble of the past returned to surround him, he didn't know if he could keep it at bay. "I definitely enjoyed that part, too."

"Well, I'll see you on Monday."

"See you Monday." Gripping the steering wheel, he held on as he watched her get out of the car and walk away from him. This was the best way for both of them. He didn't need a relationship with a woman like her and she definitely didn't need anything with a man like him. He wasn't capable of having a full relationship. He could only do temporary and it simply wasn't in her to have a casual affair, he knew that for certain. So the best thing was to let her go home alone, forget about how she had felt against him, and he would take a cold shower to wash away the demons of desire that circled around him now.

Before she closed her car door, he hurried around the front of his truck, ready to close it for her. She looked up with a startled expression that changed the instant her eyes met his. She rose from her seat and reached out to him. In seconds she was in his arms, and he kissed her again. He pressed his mouth to hers and parted her lips. Exploring, teasing, tasting, testing, he let go of any restraint, pressing her against her car. Her fragrance and the way it wrapped itself in his mind drew him closer. When her arms clutched his shoulders, he knew he could lose himself in her if he weren't careful. Each curve, each nuance of her was impressed on him for the last time and he knew it. It had to be this way.

Miguel's hard body against hers was right, and wonderful, and so masculine. There was no protest in her as he pressed her against her car. The way his mouth explored hers, the silken glide of his tongue against hers made her want more than just this embrace. The feel of his arousal revealed that he was more than able to take things to another level. She wished that she was more adventurous, but taking the lead in a relationship hadn't been her way. But surely a night in bed with Miguel would be worth any regrets she might face later?

The wind shifted and fluttered the hem of her dress against her leg, teased a tendril of her hair against her cheek and gave her a chance to catch her breath. She clutched his shoulders and hugged him against her, trying to catch her breath.

The rasp of his light beard teased the bare skin at her neck. Then the pain came, and she winced. "Ow."

"What's wrong?" Miguel stilled except for his harsh breathing.

"I think I got a little sun," she said, and placed a hand on her neck. The skin was hot to the touch, but she didn't know if it was from the sun or Miguel's influence.

"Let me see," he said, and opened her car door so the light shone on her. She bent down and Miguel eased one of the dress straps to the side. "Yep. I'd say you have sunburn that's going to get your attention tonight."

"I forgot about sunblock today." She hated sleeping with sunburn. "Does it look that bad?"

"Unfortunately. Why don't we go in the clinic and have a better look at it?"

"It'll be okay, Miguel. I ought to know better, though."

"Take a shower when you get home or a mild vinegar bath sometimes takes the sting out."

"Isn't that just old wives' tales?" she asked, smiling, liking the way he incorporated nontraditional treatments into his medical practice. That was probably from working in such a nontraditional setting.

"It's true, though."

"Okay, then, I'll give it a try." She faced him and took his hands in hers. "Even though this was a nondate, and I was just helping you out, I had a really good time. You have a wonderful family." She was a little envious of the closeness they shared. It was a far cry from the formality of hers, especially since her mother had died. Before that, things had been different.

"Thanks. I had a great time, too. One of these days you can drag me along to one of your family functions, and we'll call it even."

A snort nearly made it out of her, but she choked it down. "I'll spare you that, but maybe something else will come up." That would be the day that she voluntarily brought anyone home to meet her father. The last man she'd tried to introduce was likely scarred for life. "Anyway, I'll see you on Monday."

Miguel ran his hand over his face as if he was trying

to think of something to say, but instead he sighed. "Monday, then."

She got into her car. With what she hoped was a casual wave she drove off and left him standing there, watching her go. The cold sweat that broke out on her didn't stop until she was miles away. Just the mention of him meeting her family was enough to inspire panic, and the insecurity of the past returned. Was she doing the right thing? Would she and Miguel really have a chance at something or was this just attraction for a bad boy from the south part of town?

Slowly, she relaxed her grip on the steering wheel and let out a breath she hadn't realized she'd been holding. Miguel's family and background were so different from hers. There wasn't a likely chance that even if they tried to make something of it, they'd be successful. People gravitated to the familiar, and they were simply poles apart in that. Although she'd not kept her family name off her job application, she had considered it. For once in her life she'd just wanted to be accepted on her own merits, not the reputation her family lineage brought with it.

He wasn't far from her thoughts as she peeled her clothing off and got into the shower. His touch and his scent clung to her until she entered the shower stall. The water felt like a zillion cactus needles on her skin, piercing and poking at her, but she knew that if she could tolerate it for a little while, some of the sting would stop and her skin would be happier. After moisturizing heavily with cocoa butter, she finally got the relief she needed and the desire to sleep overwhelmed her. Crawling between the crisp, Egyptian cotton sheets on her platform bed was the most luxurious feeling. With the heat of her skin roaring like a bonfire, she settled down and closed her eyes.

The rest she craved came in bits and pieces, interrupted frequently by images of Miguel and memories of his touch.

CHAPTER EIGHT

ON MONDAY morning Vicky's nerves tightened. How would it be to work with Miguel again? Would things change or would they simply return to their work roles and forget about the stunning kisses they had shared?

Saturday seemed like a moment out of time and possibly a hallucination. If it hadn't been for the evidence burned onto her skin, she might have considered the passion between them part of her imagination or a lusty daydream.

There was only one way to find out. She had to go through the door to the clinic. Either way, she had a job to do.

"Mercy, girl!" Tilly said, and did a double take when Vicky walked into the nurses' station. "What happened to you?"

"Oh, I got some sun over the weekend," Vicky said, and tried not to let the butterflies in her stomach get away.

"I'll say. Looks like you got burned to a crisp. Are you okay?"

"Oh, yeah, I'm fine," Vicky said, and gave a quick laugh. "Just have to remember the sunblock next time."

"Be sure you do. And a hat. With your coloring, you're

at risk for skin cancer if you don't watch out." Tilly clucked her tongue then went back to the computer.

"I will. I will." The small reprimand brought back thoughts of her mother's illness. She hadn't known how her cancer had started and it certainly could have been a melanoma. Her mother had been a sun worshiper as a young woman. She really would have to be extracareful with such an unknown family history. But work first.

Mondays always seemed to be the busiest of days and this one was no different. She only had time for a cursory greeting to the other staff and a nod to Miguel before patients flooded the clinic.

Each time she passed Miguel in a patient room or discussed a case, the tension knotted tighter in her gut. He wasn't meeting her eyes, and the smile he offered to others wasn't sent her way. Things had reverted back to the way they'd been before Saturday. Maybe Saturday had been a daydream after all.

So she fell back on her nursing role and decided she'd get depressed later. Too many people depended on her giving her best right now for her to indulge in personal feelings. If she was overly bright or her smile too big, only she knew why.

The last patient of the day was a heartbreaker. Or at least she would be in about ten years or so.

The huge tears that coursed down the little girl's cheeks nearly did Vicky in. She loved children and hated to see any of them suffering. She squatted down to be at eye level with the girl and cast a quick glance at the name on her clipboard.

"What happened to you, Trina?" she asked, seeing quite well that blood oozed from a makeshift bandage her mother had applied to her injured knee.

"I fell...in the rocks," she said, her words interspersed with tearful gasps.

"I couldn't clean it up. I know there is dirt in there, but I just couldn't do it," the mother said, nearly as tearful as Trina, and pressed a hand to the bump of her belly.

"It's okay. Lots of women have sensitivities when they are pregnant." Vicky stood. "Can I pick you up, Trina, and we'll go get your knee all fixed up?"

Only a nod and more tears were the answer, but she held her arms up to Vicky.

"It's okay, darling. It'll be okay." Vicky closed her eyes as Trina's arms closed around her neck in silent trust and acceptance. For a second Vicky's breath caught. If only she had been this trusting as a child, had been encouraged to be, maybe she wouldn't have such trust issues as an adult, but the fact was that she had them. As she looked at Miguel entering the room with a bright smile, she nearly forgot to breathe again. She cleared her throat and gained control of her emotions.

Her stomach tightened when he peeled back the bandage. There certainly were bits of gravel embedded in the wound and she was going to need a few stitches for sure. "Ouch! That must have hurt," he said. "What happened, little one?"

Trina nodded and her chin began to tremble again. "I fell."

"I'm guessing irrigation and a few stitches?" Vicky asked, and patted Trina's back.

"You got it." Miguel paused, looking at how Trina clung to Vicky. "Why don't you sit with her and I'll get the supplies?"

While Miguel got ready, Vicky sat on the exam table

and brought Trina across her lap. "Just hold tight to me, darling, and this will be over before you know it."

In minutes the irrigation was over and Miguel had picked out a few remaining bits of dirt. After a quick injection of numbing medication, he was able to place a few stitches to close the wound. "That ought to do it."

When Miguel looked up, a lump formed in his throat and his heart skipped at least a few beats. Vicky sat with Trina folded across her lap. Vicky's eyes were closed, she had tucked her chin over the little girl's head and was humming softly. What a gorgeous picture they made. Vicky didn't move except to open her eyes. As her gaze held his, something stirred in him. The same something that had been stirred over the weekend when he'd held her in his arms now roared to life, but he struggled to control it. He swallowed then cleared his throat and tried to choke down the emotions that wanted to race out of him. Vicky was truly beautiful as the light of her heart shone through, but it would never be enough to bridge the gap between them. No, it was best to keep his distance. "All done here. How about a few stickers and a lollipop or two?"

Distraction. That was the ticket for Trina as well as himself. If he busied himself with the tasks at hand, he might forget the feelings Vicky brought out in him.

Vicky looked at her. "Ready now? All the nasty stuff is done." She hugged Trina. "Let's go find you a treat. You were very brave."

"I was, huh?" Trina held her leg up to look at the stitches and then back at Vicky. Tears and questions brimmed in those big brown eyes.

"It's okay. They'll only be in for a little while and

then we'll take them out when your skin grows together. Then you won't need them anymore."

"Can I have a lollipop now?" she asked.

"Absolutely, then we'll get you back to your mom."

Miguel entered his office just before the last of the staff left for the day. Vicky made sure that everyone was gone before she sealed her fate. She didn't need any witnesses to what she was about to do. Her heart thundered in her chest and her mouth went dry. Confrontation was not in her makeup, but she had to do this. Not knowing where things lay between her and Miguel was worse than knowing there was nothing. The truth might not set her free, but it could free her from unrealistic expectations and she could go on with her life.

She knocked on the doorframe and he looked up, surprise on his face, which quickly switched to a closed, guarded expression. "I thought you left with everyone else." The set of his shoulders was stiff and unyielding, unlike the way they had softened beneath her touch just days ago.

"Just had one detail to wrap up." If that's what you could call it.

"What's that?"

She entered the room and sat on the edge of the chair across from his desk. "It's about us."

"Us? There is no us, Vicky." He leaned forward and folded his hands together on top of the desk. "I'm sorry if I misled you, but any relationship between us is out of the question."

Any possible hope inside her deflated at his statement. "I see."

"I'll apologize now, because I can see with the

clarity of hindsight that my behavior on Saturday was unacceptable."

"Unacceptable?" She gave a harsh laugh. "It was perfectly acceptable at the time. What changed in the last forty-eight hours?" Bitterness sizzled on the back of her tongue.

"I did." With a sigh, he leaned back. "I realized that it was inappropriate of me to behave the way I did and give you an impression that things could be different between us." A frown covered his face. "I can see that this makes you uncomfortable, so if you were to resign, I would totally understand."

"Resign? The idea never occurred to me, Dr. Torres. I'm made of sterner stuff than that." She pulled herself upright in the chair. "I'm not going anywhere. If you don't want me to show up tomorrow, you'll have to fire me now. I simply needed to know where things stood between us and now that I know, I'll head home." She rose from the chair. "I have to say that I disagree with your position. There was something magical between us and it wasn't due to the wine."

Miguel opened his mouth then closed it again and let her go out the door. Frustration and anger at himself burned in his gut. He'd handled that as poorly as he'd handled anything in his life. There was no way he'd fire her. After being here such as short time, the other staff and patients had already begun to depend on her and asked for her when they arrived. Dammit. He was beginning to depend on her too, way more than he'd ever expected or wanted to.

He didn't need the complication of any relationship, let alone one with a coworker who happened to be from the richest family in the city. Yeah, that was just what he needed to make his life complete. What could he bring to a woman like Vicky anyway? Grief, a family history to rival any fictional account and unrelenting misery? No, the best thing was for them to maintain their professional relationship, and he'd have to forget about how remarkable she had felt in his arms.

If he could.

The rest of the week passed in a blur, with the days running together, the patients melding one into another, and finally the week ended on a particularly sour note.

Their additional funding wasn't going to come through. The city was functioning at a massive deficit and couldn't find the money to assist the clinic. It simply wasn't going to happen this year and possibly not for the next few years. Layoffs and cuts were inevitable for the city and now probably for the clinic, too.

The staff sat in the waiting area after the last patient left on Friday night. Miguel looked around at the despondent group after he'd broken the news to them.

"I'm really sorry to have to tell you all this, but I just found out that the current funding will only last us through July. The city won't come through. After that, I can't see how we're going to be able to carry on."

"You've kept this place going for years, M. You can keep it going now, can't you?" Carlos asked, his wide eyes reflecting the shock in everyone else's.

"It's not just what we do, but it's the cost of supplies, the building maintenance and rent, which has gone up in the last two years and is now expected to go up again this year." It was an endless source of frustration to him. No matter how hard he worked to keep the desperately needed clinic going, external forces seemed at odds with his plans.

"How about that private fundraiser?" Vicky asked, her eyes guarded. She was calm, but he could see that she was thinking very hard about this. "I have an idea for one that could potentially keep the clinic going for years."

"Potentially?" Miguel asked, and shook his head. "I'm sorry, Vicky, but for this we need a sure thing. These people aren't going to get paid on a 'maybe.'" He'd been disappointed so many times in the past by potential plans that never worked out. He didn't want to risk any false hope on another one. "Anyone else have a brainstorm they want to share?"

The rest of the staff perked up and there was an outcry among them. "Wait! Let's hear what the lady has to say," Carlos said. "She got us coffee and donuts, maybe she can help with this, too. You never know what kind of connections she could have."

"If there's any idea worth hearing, Miguel, I say let's hear it," Tilly said. "Come on, Vicky, what is it?"

She looked at Miguel and hesitated. He nodded. What the hell? "Okay, let's hear it."

Vicky stood and faced the small group of people she had come to know over the past month or so. They were friends now. She knew she could trust them. "Well, I've been involved in some fundraising events in the past and it's always easier to get a bunch of people to donate a small amount than it is to get fewer investors to commit to larger funds." She tucked her hair behind her left ear. "Carlos, you're partly right. My father knows some people and so does my brother. They're people who live in this city and who might be able to help us out. They simply need to know about us."

"What kind of fundraiser are you talking about? It's going to have to be big," Tilly said with a cluck of her tongue. "If we intend to save this clinic, we need a lot of money, not loose change from people's pockets."

"Insurance companies have dropped their reimbursements, the co-pays are going up and people are losing jobs, too. We all know how hard it is to make ends meet these days." She looked around at the faces in front of her and saw the desperation, the will and the strength in each of them, and she wouldn't want to let any of them, but especially Miguel, down. He'd been let down so many times that he needed someone to come through for him and she wanted to be that person, even if nothing else transpired between them. "If you can give me a couple of weeks, I can pull it together. I'm sure of it."

"We all expect you to give us jobs to do so you're not doing everything by yourself," Tilly said, and crossed her arms. "We're in this together, Vicky."

"Agreed. I'll do some preliminary planning and see what kind of numbers I can come up with then we'll go from there."

Applause broke out in the little group and Vicky couldn't keep the grin off her face. When she looked at Miguel, her heart nearly thumped its way out of her chest. The way he looked at her, the way his energy, his focus seemed to home in on her made her want to reach out to him, but he'd made his position clear.

"I'll give you two weeks. If it's not coming together by then, I think we'll need to make other plans."

Vicky stuck out her hand to Miguel. "Agreed."

"I say we head out. Not going to solve anything on a

Friday night." Tilly fished her purse from beneath her chair and stood. "See you all next week."

There was a mass exodus of staff. For once Carlos didn't have a quick solution or a flip answer. In silence he slid out the door with the rest of them.

"Hey," Miguel said. "Can you give me an idea of what you're planning? It would help me if I could know the details as soon as possible."

"Sure. What you need to do for a fundraiser like this is give the people a good time, that's all. Music, food, some dancing. People enjoy getting dressed up for a good cause. Every year there are fundraisers in town that people look forward to, like the Chocolate Fantasy Ball. Maybe we could make this the first annual one for the clinic. I haven't got it all figured out yet, but it will come together, don't worry."

"There are so many things to worry about, Vicky. You don't know how hard I worked to turn this place around. There simply isn't money to purchase the building, and I'm afraid the owner won't work out something that is in our best interests."

"Your hard work has shown, otherwise it wouldn't be so full every day, right?"

"Yes."

"And you take people with and without insurance. The simple answer may be a nonprofit status." She got excited about that idea. "My older brother is an accountant, so I'll talk to him about it, too."

Letting out a long sigh, Miguel rubbed a hand over his face. "I'm too tired to think about it right now. If you're ready, I'll walk you out."

She wanted to be able to say something to him, something that would ease his mind, but right now she didn't have the words. She would have to prove it to him. "I'm ready." She shouldered her purse and started toward the door, but they paused as it opened unexpectedly.

Carlos burst into to the clinic with a surprised look on his face.

"What, did you forget your backpack again?" Miguel said, but then some instinct, some sick feeling of dread bubbled up in him from a dark place in the past. He knew that look.

"No." Carlos held out a hand to Miguel. Blood dripped from his fingers. "I..." His eyes rolling back in his head, Carlos crumbled.

Without even thinking about it, Miguel lunged forward to catch him before he hit the floor. A wave of adrenaline hit Miguel like a tsunami. Nothing else mattered. He had to save Carlos. Thank God Vicky hadn't left yet, or he would have been more desperate than he already was.

"Carlos!" Vicky screeched, and dived to the floor opposite Miguel. "What happened?" She fumbled in her pocket for her phone.

"I don't know, but he's bleeding badly."

"I'll get 911 on the way." After a short conversation with the 911 operator, Vicky put the phone on speaker and sat it on the floor beside them to keep the line open.

Every move Miguel made felt as if it was being made in slow motion and he were shrinking away into the past. Every instinct he possessed as a physician and a healer kicked in to overdrive, but seeing Carlos on the floor nearly paralyzed him. This scene was so familiar it sickened him and brought back the night that had forever changed him.

"What are his injuries?" Vicky asked, and snapped on a pair of gloves.

"I don't know. He's got blood on his shirt." So much about Carlos reminded him of his brother. Until now, he hadn't realized it. Looking down at Carlos was like looking down at Emilio dying in his arms again. Reaching out toward the shirt, his arms locked and his hands trembled.

"Miguel? Miguel!" Vicky reached out and shook his arm. "Whatever is going on inside you right now has to be put aside. We have to focus on Carlos."

The sound of her voice pulled him from the past and with a monumental effort he shoved away the images of his dead brother. Vicky reached out and pushed the shirt up to expose Carlos's torso.

CHAPTER NINE

THE sight of a knife wound below the left rib cage stirred Miguel to action. There was a similar wound above his navel. "Dammit." The blood flow from the larger wound was a dreadful sign. "He's been cut deep, possibly the spleen." That alone was life-threatening.

"I'll get the cart." Vicky rushed into the trauma room and brought out the crash cart. "Everything we need is in here. We'll save him, Miguel. We'll save him."

Despite her brave words, he heard the tremor in her voice. She was as uncertain as he.

"Get a couple of big lines in him and all the fluid you got. He needs blood and surgery." He reached up, snapped opened the drawer with dressing supplies in it and grabbed a handful of gauze. Applying pressure to the wound externally wasn't going to help much when the injury was likely as deep as the spleen, but he had to do something. Dammit, there was so little that they could do.

"Get some oxygen going, too," Vicky said, without looking up from the IV she had just put into Carlos's right arm. In seconds she had fluids going and was reaching for his left arm to put another in. Then she paused, hope surfacing in her eyes. "I know it's not much, but what about a tampon?"

"A tampon?" Miguel frowned, dumbfounded.

"I read about marines using them for field dressings."

In that instant Miguel saw exactly where she was going with that thought. The expansion of a tampon deep inside the wound could provide some internal pressure that might slow down the bleeding and absorb some of the blood. "Do you have any?"

"Purse." She put in the second IV.

Miguel grabbed her handbag, turned it upside down and shook everything out of it. He grabbed the three tampons that surfaced. "You'll have to do it. I don't know how to operate these things."

Without a word, Vicky handed the IV bags to Miguel and ripped open a tampon pack. With deft fingers, she inserted a tampon into the edge of the larger wound.

"Go deeper."

Vicky's trembling hands pushed the tampon an inch or two farther. "You have to push the tampon bit forward with the applicator." After that, Miguel used his gauze to mop up the blood that had leaked out. The flow slowed to a trickle.

He grinned, now feeling as if there was real hope for Carlos. "You did it!"

Sirens cut the stifling air between them and the crews from an ambulance and fire emergency crashed through the front doors. The silence and isolation was fractured as new energy and people with purpose poured around them. The overwhelming relief that flashed through Miguel was a kind he'd never known. Now the tremors began in his gut and in his limbs. "He's been stabbed, possibly into the spleen. Lots of bleeding."

"Has he roused?" the paramedic in charge asked, while the others tended to Carlos, taking over each task from Vicky and applying oxygen at a higher concentration.

"He walked in then lost consciousness right away."

"Did he hit the floor?"

"I caught him so he didn't hit his head." Miguel tugged on his lab coat then realized it was covered in blood and tore it off. "Look, I'll go with you and answer questions, but this kid needs blood, stat."

"We'll get him loaded, Doc."

The next few minutes were a flurry of activity as they loaded the still-unconscious Carlos onto a stretcher and hurried out the door with him.

As Miguel was about to step into the back of the ambulance, Vicky called to him. "Will you call his mother?" she asked, tears now rolling down her face. Worry clouded her eyes, but he couldn't take the time to comfort her now. He had to save Carlos first.

"I'll call her. Come to the E.R. after us." He needed her comforting presence with him. He was selfish enough to admit that.

"Go! I'll catch up."

The ambulance doors slammed shut and Miguel's last image of Vicky was of her racing across the parking lot to her car.

When Vicky found Miguel, he was sitting in a chair outside the surgery waiting room, his elbows on his knees, his face in his hands. He looked like a man filled with anguish. At first she hesitated, not sure whether to disturb his solitude, then something snapped inside her. He'd been alone too long.

She rushed to him and dropped to her knees. "Miguel." She threw her arms around his shoulders. "They've taken him to surgery already?"

"Yes."

After a second's hesitation his arms flashed out around her. She felt the desperation in them and clung to him harder, trying to infuse as much of her energy and comfort into him as she could. "Tell me."

"It's his spleen for sure and possibly a major vessel. The other one is uncertain."

"I'm so sorry. Oh, God, I'm so sorry." For a second or two they simply held each other, sharing their grief over their young friend. "Did you call his family?"

"They'll be here in a few minutes." Miguel pulled back from her but kept her between his knees.

"You love him like a brother, don't you?" She could see the agony in his eyes and knew it was true. Though she didn't know much about his past, she knew he'd lost his own brother.

"Yes. He's like the little brother I had and lost. His mother is my mother's best friend, so we've known each other a long, long time. If it hadn't been for that crazy tampon trick of yours, he would have died right in front of us." His eyes glittered but she didn't know if it was anger or from tears he couldn't allow himself to shed.

A puff of air escaped her throat and tears overflowed her eyes. "I don't know whether to laugh or cry about that."

"I don't either, but you certainly saved his life."

Vicky placed her hands on his face and made him look at her. She was no saint. "*We* saved his life. Together.

Now it's up to God and the surgeons." She sniffed. "We can only pray and send good energy for him."

Nodding, Miguel pressed his face into the junction of her neck and shoulder. Tremors rolled through him, and he held on to her. For the first time she felt as if he truly needed her and she reveled in that sensation. And she knew that she certainly needed him. It wasn't the heat of the moment, it wasn't simply passion that came and went. She was falling in love with him. With everything she had in her, she was falling for him.

Tears coursed down her face as they held each other, oblivious to the noise of the hallway around them. The goings-on of the hospital simply ebbed and flowed around them. Together they were solid as a rock, and there was no separating them. If only she could convince Miguel of it.

Then chaos, the likes of which she'd never seen, descended on them. Cries of alarm and hysterical Spanish mixed with equally hysterical English bombarded them, and they drew apart. "Family's here," Miguel said, and stood, then pulled her to her feet. He kept her by his side until Carlos's mother separated herself from the group of people surrounding them.

Miguel didn't have to introduce them. Vicky knew from the tone of her voice and the tears rushing down her face that this was Carlos's mother. She was the matriarch of this family and everyone deferred to her.

Rushing forward, she nearly threw herself at Miguel. He held her and listened. With the smattering of Spanish that she knew, Vicky heard words that she understood, but she couldn't quite put it all together and she took a step back as the group surged around Miguel. In minutes they had calmed down a little, and Miguel switched to

English. "He's in surgery now and is going to need lots of blood."

An immediate outcry came to donate for their brother, their cousin, their friend.

"Good idea. Some of you can go down to the blood bank right now. Tell them you want to give blood for a patient in surgery, then come back up and wait while some others of you do the same."

Vicky's gaze flashed to Miguel and she frowned, but didn't say anything. She knew that wasn't quite a correct interpretation, but he had to have reasons for making that statement.

"Vicky, this is Carlos's mother, Priscilla."

Before she knew what had happened, she found herself enveloped in a hug from Carlos's mother. Surprise made her eyes go wide then her arms went around the tearful woman. *"Gracias, gracias, gracias!"* She took a breath and pulled back from Vicky. "Miguel tells me of what you did to save *mijo.* Tampons, of all things!" She shook her head in disbelief. "You are truly an angel to save my son."

"Oh, but, really, Miguel—"

"He is an angel, too," she said. She patted Vicky's cheek and held a hand out to Miguel, bringing him closer. "The two of you will ever be in my prayers. Thank you. Thank you." She held her arms out to the two of them, and the family crowded around, adding their love and thanks.

Never in her life had she felt such an overpowering sense of love and purpose. Although she was sorry about Carlos's injury, it certainly proved to her that she was where she needed to be and this was the kind of work she was meant to do. It didn't matter where she had been born, or how she had lived her life previously—this moment in time clarified it all.

"You're welcome seems so silly to say right now." She sniffed and wiped her cheek on a shoulder.

"It's not silly at all." Priscilla pulled herself upright and nodded. "You are right. Now is the time to be strong for Carlos. Thank you again, *hija*. I will always be indebted to you."

"Oh, no—"

"Please, *hija?* Allow me that?"

Vicky paused and looked at the faces of Carlos's family around her. They needed this, and she could give it to them. Nodding, she hugged Priscilla then moved to the background.

A few minutes later, after some of the family had left for the blood bank in the basement of the hospital, Miguel sat beside her. "You okay?"

"Yeah, sure." She offered a smile, but inside she was a mass of nerves. Clutching her hands in her lap, she tried to focus on something else. "How long do you think he'll be in surgery?"

"At least another hour. Getting the spleen out is first then checking the other areas for injury will take a while." Without another word Miguel leaned back in the chair, placed an arm around her shoulders and pulled her against him.

For a second she resisted, then the emotion and the energy of the past hour or so caught up to her and she nearly melted.

"Do you know how he got stabbed in the first place? It hadn't occurred to me until now."

"No. We'll have to wait until he wakes up to find out. Even then he may not have any memory of the attack itself, just vague splotches of images. The brain protects us that way."

"Is that what you told his mother?"

"Yes. And as far as I know, it's the truth." His lips pressed together and there was a tension about him.

"But you have an idea, don't you?"

Miguel leaned toward her, cupped a hand on her left cheek and pulled her face closer to his. "I don't want to say anything with the family so close." He pulled back and placed a quick kiss on her forehead.

Nodding as he pulled back, she looked up, wishing that he would kiss her once more but afraid that she wasn't ever going to experience that again. Without thinking, she placed a hand on the back of his neck and closed the distance between them. It was only a chaste kiss on the lips, but one she needed to give him. "It's going to be okay, Miguel. It's going to be okay." Somehow she knew Carlos was going to pull through. "He's young and strong. He'll make it."

As he drew back, he took her hand in his and pressed a long kiss to her palm.

Some of the family returned from the blood bank and others went down to donate their blood. Everyone settled down into a somber group as they waited for the surgeons to give a report on Carlos's condition.

Two hours later, the surgical team, two male physicians, both of whom wore exhausted expressions, entered the waiting room. "Carlos's family?" one of them asked. Even before he finished looking around, the two men were surrounded by Carlos's eager relatives.

"He'll make it."

Cheers and tears erupted in the room. It was exactly

what they wanted and needed to hear. Miguel reached out for Vicky and brought her against his side. He needed her there. At least for the moment he needed her. He'd allow himself to lean on her for a while then he'd stand on his own, as he always had.

Then her trembling touch and her fragrance wrapped themselves around him tight and he didn't know if he could ever let her go. Turning to face her, he held her even more tightly, allowing himself that indulgence.

"He's got a good heart, a young healthy body and an extreme run of good luck," the surgeon said to the group, then his gaze came to rest on Miguel. "Miguel? What are you doing here?"

Miguel moved forward, with Vicky still clinging to his side. He shook the surgeon's hand. "Hello, Craig. It's been a long time. Carlos is my employee…and a very good friend." His voice broke and he cleared his throat.

"I'm so sorry to have run into you this way," Craig said.

Miguel nodded and introductions were made. "I'm assuming he's headed for the surgical ICU?"

"Yes. He's doing well in Recovery, but we'll keep him sedated for the first twenty-four hours or so and limit visitors to immediate family only."

"Understood. He needs to hear his mama's voice."

Priscilla stepped forward with authority and held out both of her hands to the surgeons. "I'm his mother. Thank you both for saving my son's life."

Craig grinned. "You're welcome. We did the clean-up job, but whoever thought of the tampon trick really saved his life long enough for us to get the rest of the job done."

Priscilla turned to Miguel and Vicky and nodded. "It was those two."

Vicky turned a glorious shade of red and tried to move behind Miguel, but he wasn't having any of it. "Come out here, you, and accept the credit you deserve. It was brilliant."

"But I didn't do anything," she muttered, and her eyes were wide with panic.

"Don't ever say that, *mija,*" Priscilla said. "You did save my son's life and for that I'll never forget it."

"Absolutely," Craig said. "The tampon expanded fast enough and applied enough compression internally to slow the bleeding. That couldn't have been accomplished with simple external pressure." He gave a chuckle and the tension in the room loosened its grip. "I think I'll ask the ambulance crews to stock tampons from now on."

Vicky looked up at Miguel, helpless, and then she burst out laughing. The family joined her as she covered her face with her hands.

CHAPTER TEN

SHE looked so beautiful standing there with the flush on her face and surrounded by people who had been strangers but, due to her selfless actions, were now lifelong friends. And against his will Miguel was falling hard and fast for her. Much more than he'd ever thought possible. Guarding against the enticing Vicky Sterling-Thorne was much harder than he'd expected. She was so much more than he had thought in the beginning. Now he was going to have to rethink his beliefs.

Arrangements were made for Priscilla and Carlos's father to have visits in the ICU; other family members were sent home to start cooking. Relatives and friends were going to arrive at the house, and having a pot of beans and rice, as well as one full of *posolé,* a stew of pork or lamb and hominy, would feed everyone. At times like this the family came together.

The midnight hour approached, and Miguel felt the exhaustion of the day crowding in on his mind. Fatigue like he hadn't felt since his residency weighed his shoulders down.

"Arc you ready to go?" Vicky asked. "I can give you a lift home. Seems like everyone else has settled down now."

Unfortunately, one could function on adrenaline only for so long before one's body crashed. Miguel was on the crashing end now, and he knew it. If he didn't get home soon, he was going to keel over. "Yes. If you don't mind, I'd love a ride home."

"I don't mind at all." They said their goodbyes and in minutes were in Vicky's car on the nearly empty streets, headed west from the University of New Mexico Hospital. Silence filled the air between them, but Miguel reached over and took her right hand, needing just that little bit of a last connection between them. When he got home and they returned to work, the closeness between them would end. Again.

He directed her through the residential neighborhood to a small cul-de-sac that was almost hidden by sprawling oak trees nearly as old as the city itself. His bungalow was at the end of another property. "It started out as a caretaker's cottage or a mother-in-law's quarters or something. I bought it about five years ago."

"It's darling. Pretty similar to the house I live in. It was a caretaker's cottage a long time ago, too, but when I divorced my husband I took it over."

Miguel unbuckled his seat belt, but didn't have the energy to open the door just yet. "I didn't realize you were divorced. Not that it's my business."

"No problem. It was a mistake from the get-go, but I corrected it as soon as I realized what was going on."

"What do you mean?"

"I married a man who took his money to bed instead of his wife. Ambition and greed didn't leave any room for me." She snorted. "That still burns. I should have seen it sooner."

"At least you saw it."

"Yeah. Want me to walk you up?" she asked, changing the subject. The green glow of the instrument panel illuminated her face, and he could see the little smile flirting with her lips.

"I know it's late, but would like you like a cup of coffee or something before you head home? I know neither of us had dinner and I won't be able to settle down for hours."

"If all you have is instant coffee, I'll pass. I can grab something at home."

He patted her knee. "Come on. I'll fix you a sandwich or something."

While Miguel puttered around the kitchen, Vicky wandered the hallway with the glass of wine he'd poured for her and admired the photographs on the walls. "These are just gorgeous, Miguel. You do have a beautiful family."

"Thanks," he said. "There's a whole pile of pictures I need to put up, but just never seem to find the time to do it."

"More cousins?"

"Yes. My mother has eight siblings, my father nine, and I have four."

Vicky's eyes widened. "Wow. There's just my two brothers and I. Only the older brother has kids, two. The younger has his own business he's married to, so I doubt there will be any children from that union."

Miguel laughed. "Let's hope not." He pushed a sandwich on a paper plate over the breakfast bar toward her and together they sat on the bar stools and ate with their hands. There was something simple yet incredibly exotic about eating plain food with the hands.

As he watched Vicky pull grapes off the small bunch

he'd given her, he found himself becoming aroused at the sight of her small fingers holding the fruit as if it were fragile then pressing a kiss to each grape before she put it in her mouth.

"Why are you doing that?"

"Doing what?"

"Giving each grape a kiss?" He watched her hands as she plucked another grape.

"I didn't realize I was. I must be tired. It was something that I heard of as a kid, giving thanks to the goddess of the vine for the bountiful harvest, or something like that," she said, and waved away the sentiment. "It's silly, I know, but it never hurts to give thanks."

"I like it." He pulled a grape from his own plate, kissed it and held it out to her. Her gaze flashed to him, suspicious yet curious, brimming with desire. Hesitation in every movement, she leaned forward and accepted the grape from his outstretched fingers. The soft touch of her lips against his skin inflamed his arousal.

Without taking her eyes away from him, she picked up a grape from her plate, kissed it then held it out to him. "I think they taste better this way. What do you think?"

A growl burned deep in him. It was animal instinct, something wild and untamed that he'd kept locked up for too long. He circled her wrist with his hand and took the grape from her fingers. Its sweet, tangy flavor nearly exploded in his mouth. "It is better." He moved closer to her. "I wonder if it's the same."

"What's the same?" Her gaze flashed to his mouth. She knew he wanted to kiss her, and she was obviously not displeased with the notion.

"If I kiss *you* and then eat a grape. Will it taste the

same?" He edged a little closer to her, drawing her closer by her wrist.

"The only real way to tell is by testing, right?" She licked her lips, her breathing shallow and rapid, and allowed him to pull her closer, until only inches separated them.

"That would be the only proper scientific análysis."

Science couldn't wait for the answer and neither could Miguel. He closed the tiny gap between them, brought her lithe body against him and pressed his mouth to her parted lips. Heat seared him everywhere he touched her. Her skin, her hair, her breasts burned into him, and her hips tight against him roused him further.

It was the fresh, fruity taste of her that finally unchained the man-beast inside him. The taste of her silky tongue against his, infused with the freshness of the grape, blended with her own, made him want to throw away any personal ethics and strip her bare right then.

Her arms wound around his shoulders and held him tight. Each move she made renewed the scent of her in his mind and turned the key to the primitive male held captive inside him. He hadn't felt this moved by a woman in so long. She was precious and kind, and lovely beyond measure.

And he didn't deserve her. That was the problem.

He ended the kiss and hugged her tight. Her breathing was just as rapid as his and he could feel the way their hearts raced in time, as if they beat as one in separate bodies. If he weren't who he was and if circumstances had been different, they might have made a go of this thing simmering between them. But he wasn't, and they couldn't. It was that simple. The words *if only* echoed through his heart and his soul.

"Grape?" she asked, and pulled back.

"What?" he blinked and tried to refocus on her.

"To finish the experiment, we need to eat a grape."

"Oh, yes. Right." Putting more space between them, he sat in his chair. He took a grape and handed her one. "Cheers."

"I'd say it's a hit and if it gets out, it might catch on worldwide."

He laughed. "You are such a nut." Then the smile faded away. "This has been a pretty crazy day, hasn't it?"

"That's the understatement of the year." She pushed her hair back from her face. "I can't think of a time I used up so much adrenaline in one day. I sure hope Carlos is going to be okay."

"Me, too." They were both aware of the ramifications of what could set in. ARDS, adult respiratory distress syndrome, could also hit him and make his recovery slower or permanently change him.

"I have to ask you, though, why did you send the family to the blood bank? The blood they donated wouldn't be used for Carlos. It has to be donated ahead of time, but you knew that."

Unable to resist the allure of her skin, he allowed his hand to stroke her cheek. "I knew. Carlos was going to use a lot of blood during surgery and possibly afterward, but the family needed something to do. It was a good way to fill up the blood bank's resources, too. I'm sure they were thrilled."

"I'm sure they were." She nodded. "It was a good thing to suggest. If you hear of any changes, let me know, okay?" She stood.

"I will."

"My brother is dragging me out to a formal dinner tomorrow night, so leave me a message if I don't answer."

"Your brother? It's okay to tell me if you have a date, Vicky. I don't have any claim on you." As his hands clenched, he tried to keep his face calm, keep the insane flash of jealousy hidden. He had no rights to Vicky. But, damn, he wanted them.

"Really, it's my brother Eddy. He's the one married to his work and doesn't take time for a social life. Once in a while he talks me into feeling sorry for him, so I go."

She shrugged, and he believed her. So many times in the past he'd been around women who thought nothing of lying to the man they were supposed to be involved with. That self-protective instinct had stuck with him over the years, but now he relaxed, trusting that Vicky was telling the truth. The warmth that hummed through him had nothing to do with fatigue and everything to do with the realization that she wasn't dating anyone else.

"I know you're tired, but try to have a good time."

She stood. "I'll try. If it weren't so late I'd try to find him a date. After tonight I'm exhausted."

"Maybe the outing will perk you up. You never know."

"I hope it's certainly less stimulating than today has been." A yawn overcame her, and she covered her mouth with one hand. "I guess I should head home now."

Miguel walked her to her car, the warm feeling lingering in his middle and migrating upward toward his heart. He knew he could never make a claim on Vicky, but he was glad that she wasn't dating anyone else. "I'll see you on Monday." He allowed himself to cup her face and bring her close for a small, chaste kiss. "Thank you for being there."

"You're welcome." She hesitated a moment, as if she wanted to say something, but didn't. He could see the questions surfacing in her eyes, and he knew he couldn't answer them. He didn't know what the hell was going on between them or how it was all going to pan out. He just knew he wanted more than he deserved.

CHAPTER ELEVEN

MIGUEL knew he had to do it, that there was no one else who could do it. His hands and his insides trembled as he unlocked the door to the clinic late Sunday morning.

The blood was still there.

The floor was covered with Carlos's blood.

The door opened against the pressure of his hand and he stepped inside, trying to control his breathing, but his heartbeat was unstoppable.

It was a mirror image of the night his brother had died.

Miguel had been determined to get Emilio out of the gang, which had been just as determined to keep him. The leader, Juan, was a kid he'd known all his life and one that had been in trouble as long as Miguel had known him. The brothers had fought earlier in the day and Emilio had run off in a rage. It seemed that the forces of the universe had been at odds that day, as well. Nothing had come together to help him and nothing had helped him save his younger brother.

Trying to ignore the rage building inside him, Miguel dragged the mop and bucket from the storage closet. He filled the bucket with steaming-hot water, added detergent and began the mop-up job. Back and forth, back and forth he went across the pool of Carlos's blood, which had dried on the floor. With each stroke of the mop memories poured into him, reminding him again of how he had failed to protect his brother and failed his family. He was the oldest. He was supposed to take care of Emilio. Even though he was a successful physician now and his clinic thrived, part of him would always be a failure.

If he hadn't tried to control Emilio, tried to force Juan to let go of his brother, Emilio might now be alive. Emilio had come home to find Miguel when Miguel had gone to find Juan. The gang leader hadn't been hard to locate. Miguel had known the neighborhood.

Emilio had arrived just as Juan had been about to put a bullet in his, Miguel's, back. Instead, Emilio had taken the slug that had been meant for him.

Everything had happened in unreal slow motion. He'd heard Emilio's warning too late. He'd turned, seen Emilio dive for Juan and they'd both fallen to the ground.

Emilio hadn't got up. In his mind, Miguel raced to where Emilio lay on the ground, a puddle of his blood pooling rapidly beneath him. The cheap white tiles on the floor had contrasted sharply with the blood.

Fear of that kind had never touched Miguel before. He'd slid to the slippery floor beside Emilio and turned him over.

"There! He's out of the gang. Now get his carcass off my floor," Juan had said.

"He needs help!" Miguel had cried, with tears of rage in his eyes. "Call 911."

"Get out." Two of Juan's assistants had hoisted Emilio up and dragged him out to the sidewalk. Though Miguel had wanted to kill Juan with his bare hands, he'd knelt beside his brother and gathered him into his arms. Even though he'd barely started medical school, he'd known that Emilio was dying, and had cursed himself for not being able to save his brother.

"Tell Mama…s-s-s-orry," Emilio had whispered, and then had closed his eyes for the last time.

The power of the memory overwhelmed Miguel, and he had to stop, close his eyes and take a minute before the images, the memory of his failure faded away. If he hadn't tried to force Emilio out of the gang, he might still be alive. But they would never know if he could have gotten out on his own.

Returning to the task, Miguel cleaned up the last of Carlos's blood, took the mop out to the Dumpster and threw it away.

Miguel arrived at the trauma-surgical ICU at the University Hospital and let himself in through the staff entrance. He'd done his resident training there and knew all of the ins and outs, the hidden exits and corridors for the staff to get around without being seen.

Although he knew and loved Carlos's family, he was still too raw to talk with anyone right now. He just needed to see Carlos and find out his condition, maybe find out what the hell had happened to him.

He opened the door from the stairwell and entered the SICU. Busy activity never stopped in a place like this. The lifeblood of the unit was the pace set, the energy, the ability for the staff to act immediately and save the next life that rolled through their doors.

Breathing deeply, he tried to suck in some of that atmosphere, that energy, and realized that he missed it, that he'd once been part of a unit like this, been part of the team that lived and thrived on emergencies. For a second he soaked it all in and good memories of his time there flooded over him. He'd once wanted to save the universe one sick patient at a time, and trauma had been his chosen method until the clinic in his community had called out to him for help. It had been a call he hadn't been able to ignore, but now he wished there was room in his life for more.

"Miguel!" A male voice brought him out of his reminiscences. "What the hell are you doing here, buddy?" The tall man dressed in surgical scrubs headed toward him, smiling widely.

"Jason!" Miguel held out his hand to the old friend striding toward him as a surge of warmth pulsed through him. "I sure didn't expect to see you still here."

"Can't pry me away." They shook hands and moved to the side of the hallway to allow staff to move past them. "What are you doing here?"

Miguel explained the situation with Carlos. "I'm responsible for the kid, and I need to know firsthand what's going on with him." It was way more than that, but he didn't want to go into any more detail at the moment.

"Just so happens he's doing great. Extubated this morning, breathing well on his own, no signs of ARDS, so I'd say he's on the mend, barring unexpected infection."

"That's great news." The tightness in Miguel's shoulders loosened and the relief pulsing through him was nearly tangible.

"He was awake a while ago, but I'm not sure now. Want to see him?"

"It's enough just to know he's been awake." The relief inside him was overwhelming.

"I hear your clinic's doing well. Still working for you?" Jason had always been observant and somehow had his finger on the pulse of gossip everywhere in this town.

"Most of the time." Miguel looked around at the bright lights of the unit and listened for a second to the rhythm beating a low hum. "I do miss this once in a while. I never realized how much until now."

"It's always been in your blood." Jason grinned. "All you have to do is apply and you can be back here in a month."

"The clinic—"

"Will run just fine if someone else takes over for you. Someone who is heading toward retirement, not a young surgeon with a passion like yours." He patted Miguel on the shoulder. "Carlos is in room fifteen. I've got to roll now, but think about it." He fished a business card out of his pocket. "Call me and let's go have a coffee."

"I will." Miguel took the card and stuck it in his pocket, wondering if he really would. When he'd left the hospital to take over the clinic, he hadn't thought he'd ever return. Now, taking in the sights and sounds around him, he wondered if that decision was written in stone.

He moved toward room fifteen, anticipating what he'd see there. Seeing patients hooked up to tubing and drains was one thing, seeing a loved one in the same position was quite another. After just a quick look inside the room he could see that Carlos had his eyes closed, that his breathing was even and deep. The monitor displayed good vital signs and the tension in Miguel's shoulders eased another notch.

Dropping into the chair beside the bed, he let go of his emotional stranglehold and rested his face on his hands, his elbows resting on his knees.

Minutes passed as he sat there, listening to the monitors and being reassured by the consistent rhythm. The nurse came and went, but didn't disturb him. Jason must have given a heads-up to the staff that it was okay for him to stay.

Footsteps entered then stopped close by him. He figured it was the nurse again, and he remained in his position, not wanting to talk to anyone just yet. The touch of a hand on his back startled him, and he looked up. Vicky stood beside him, concern etched on her face. "What are you doing here?" he asked.

"I came to see Carlos. The nurse couldn't give me any information on the phone, so I came down to talk to the family and get an update." She glanced away. "You didn't answer your phone, so I figured you might be down here."

"I turned it off when I came in." He'd actually forgotten about it. "Are you okay?"

"Me? I'm fine, but you look like death warmed over. Did you get any sleep last night?"

"Not much." He stood and moved away a little from her. If he touched her, he was going to regret it. Although her concern for him was genuine, he couldn't tolerate the honesty in her touch right now. "I'm fine. You needn't be concerned about me."

A guarded look came into her eyes, and he knew he'd hurt her. "I'll be concerned about whom I wish." She cleared her throat and stood up a little straighter. "I've come about Carlos, so can you tell me how he's doing? Priscilla said he was off the ventilator, so that's very good news."

"Yes. He's breathing on his own. I've been sitting here for a while, but he's been sleeping the whole time."

"Sleep is restorative, and he sure needs it."

"Not…sleeping," Carlos said in a voice that crackled with dryness and fatigue.

Miguel spun around and leaned over the bed. "Hey, are you in there?" he asked, and placed his hand on Carlo's forehead, needing to touch him, to have that connection to the young man who meant so much to him.

"Yeah." He licked his lips and his eyelids fluttered.

Automatically, Vicky reached for the mouth sponge to moisten his lips and tongue. "Here you go. This ought to help."

"Do you know what happened to you?" Miguel asked.

"Mugging." He paused again. "Tried to help."

"Oh, Carlos," Vicky said, and tears ran down her face. "I'm so very glad you're still with us."

"That bad?" he asked, and looked at Miguel.

"Yeah." He didn't have to say anything else. Carlos had been around enough to know what that meant.

"Thanks." He glanced at both of them.

A sudden shock of pure joy shot through him. The kid was going to be okay. Somehow he knew it. "Vicky's the one who really saved your life."

"I did not! Will you quit giving me all the credit?" The flush on her neck gave away her pleasure, despite her words.

Miguel told Carlos what had happened and how the events had unfolded.

Carlos groaned and closed his eyes.

"Are you in pain? Do you need pain medication?" Vicky asked.

"A *tampon?* You let her put a *tampon* in me?" He paused for a breath. "I'm never going to live that down."

"At least you'll live long enough to not live it down, bro." Relief continued to overwhelm Miguel.

The nurse entered the room. "Sorry, folks. Time to rest up again," she said.

"It's okay. We've spent too long with him anyway." Miguel clasped Carlos's hand. "I'll see you soon."

"I'm so glad you're on the mend," Vicky said, and pressed a kiss to his forehead. "When you're taking fluids, I'll bring you some coffee."

"The good stuff." A sideways smile lifted one corner of his mouth and his eyes drifted down.

CHAPTER TWELVE

MONDAY morning was full of the blues. Everyone, staff and patients, at the clinic knew and loved Carlos. The mood was somber as they moved through their normal clinic duties without him.

"It's just not the same without that boy, is it?" Tilly asked during the silent lunch break in the staff room. There was an almost palpable heaviness in the air, anticipating word from the family, the waiting time.

"No, it isn't," Vicky said, as her appetite for her sandwich fled. She returned it to its wrapper and covered it up. Nothing was going to make her take another bite of that unfortunate excuse for a meal that she had made. If she couldn't make a proper sandwich, she was in sad shape. After the busy week, then the horrible incident with Carlos and then the very late night with her brother and his awful dinner engagement, no one would blame her if she was exhausted.

"There's a different vibe in the air when he's here." The older woman shook her head and looked away.

Vicky knew there were tears in Tilly's eyes. She'd heard the emotion in her voice and sympathized with her, but Vicky had had a bit longer to get used to the idea and to see Carlos for herself. Seeing him in person was different than simply getting a report about him.

"How about I order us all something for lunch?" Vicky said, and tossed her sandwich bag in the trash. "This isn't cutting it for me today."

"What did you have in mind?" Tilly asked, but the other staff in the lounge looked at her, too. Since she had suggested the idea, she was in charge of it.

"How about lunch burritos or something? I'll call in the order and go get some if anyone else wants to join in. My treat for today." The idea of it was suddenly much more appealing than anything she'd thought of all day long.

"Yeah, let's do it." Tilly balled up her lunch and tossed it, as well.

With a grin, Vicky grabbed some paper for everyone to write down what they wanted. In minutes her list was complete, with the exception of Miguel's order. He had closeted himself in his office. She knocked lightly in case he was on the phone.

"Come in."

Fatigue sounded heavy in his voice, and she was sorry it was there. Carlos's condition weighed heavily on him. "We're just sending out an impromptu lunch order and wanted to know if you want in on it, my treat." She handed him the takeout menu.

"Sure." He quickly scanned it, then handed it back. "I know this place. Give me a number five with extra cheese."

She took the menu back and looked at it. "Sounds good. Might have to try that myself sometime." As she turned to go, she hesitated. "Are you okay?"

"Yes."

"I mean really okay." She bit her lip and glanced away for a second. "You seem a little off today, but considering the last few days that's not totally unreasonable."

A sideways smile crossed his mouth briefly. "Don't worry about me, Vicky. I'll be fine."

This was a level of coolness she'd never seen from him. He'd totally pulled back from the closeness they'd started to have, even as coworkers. Maybe she had been wrong again. Maybe her judgment of men hadn't improved over the years and Miguel was just like the rest of them. Couldn't be trusted to have an honest relationship. "I see. Sorry to bother you. I'll just go get this and be right back."

She closed the door behind her and huffed out a deep breath. Whatever she had once thought possible between them was now obviously just a mistaken desire. Men who ran hot and cold with their emotions unnerved her, and she couldn't deal with the dishonesty of it. Tears clouded her vision on the way to the restaurant, and she had to pull over for a minute or risk getting into an accident.

Somehow she managed to get to the restaurant, pick up the order and return to the clinic without causing an accident or dropping the bags of lunch burritos. The cheery smile she pasted on her face was a farce and she knew it, but the staff responded and that was the important thing.

The food was a big hit and after consuming the fragrant and flavorful burritos, everyone returned to work with a bit more zip in their step.

"A little green chili goes a long way, doesn't it?" Tilly asked.

"What?" Vicky blinked.

"Just look at everyone. Back to their usual selves mostly. A little green chili helped. That was a great idea you had," she said, and squeezed Vicky's arm. "We all needed it."

"It's okay. It really wasn't anything." Somehow the morose atmosphere seemed to have lightened around her, but Vicky's heart still felt heavy.

"Yes, it was, girl. It was a great idea and it's time you accepted something." Tilly turned to face her fully, making Vicky feel as if she was back in nursing school.

"What's that?"

"You're a part of this group. You might have come here as an outsider, a stranger, but you've quickly been accepted as one of us here." Then Tilly smiled.

"I don't know, Tilly. Sometimes I feel like I'm at home here and other times I just think I'll always be an outsider no matter where I go." That was the bald truth of it.

"We all feel that way at times, but, just so you know, you're one of us." Tilly patted her arm. "Now, go and get the first three patients lined up or Miguel will toss us out on our ears."

Vicky laughed, her heart a little lighter, and called for the first three patients. She placed them in different rooms, and began the assessments for Miguel.

CHAPTER THIRTEEN

THE London Broil was fabulous as always, but it didn't matter what the chef served, it always stuck in her throat. Washing the meal down with more wine didn't make it any more palatable and simply wasted good wine. The only time she thought she was developing esophageal reflux disease was at her father's dinner table.

"Victoria's got some news," Edward said as he cut into his food.

The hair on Vicky's head actually stood on end. No matter how old she was, she'd always feel six years old when she sat at her father's formal dining table. Even though it had been in the family for generations, it would always be *his* table.

Turning his head, peppered with steel-gray hair, and focusing those brilliant blue eyes on her, Charles Sterling-Thorne raised his brows at his only daughter. "What sort of news, Victoria? Did you finally come to your senses and leave that ridiculous *career* of yours? It's about time."

"Hardly, Father. I'll always be a nurse." She nearly scoffed, but managed to choke it back. Insubordination was not tolerated at the table. "Eddy's referring to something else entirely." Managing to look calm and cool on the outside had always seen her through these tense meals, but now she knew the brittle veneer was beginning to crack.

"Edward," her brother snarled at her through gritted teeth. "She's talking about having a fundraiser for her little clinic. Seems their benefactor has died, and the rest of the family is too greedy to continue the endowments."

"Well, that's too bad," her father said, his eyes glittering with amusement and his I-told-you-so look. "Guess you'll have to quit now, won't you?"

That did it. She'd tolerated his snide comments and superior looks for too many years, allowing him to control her for most of her life. It ended there and right now. Carefully, she placed her fork on the table beside the plate rimmed in gold, wiped her mouth with the linen napkin and stood.

"Victoria, sit down. The meal isn't over."

"But I am, Father. I am through with this..." She gestured to all of them and the air. "This farce of a family."

"What are you talking about? You're overreacting again as usual. Sit down." He dismissed her with his eyes and returned to his meal.

"No, it's well past time I reacted this way and stood up for myself. You will never, *ever* again belittle me or my chosen career. I am a nurse, and a damned good one. Last Friday one of our staff nearly died, and I saved his life by using my brain and not waiting for someone else to swoop in and save the day. *I* did it. *I* worked with Miguel, and together we saved this young man's life." She sniffed. "I'm very, very proud of the work I do."

Tears of rage at her father and pride in herself clouded

her vision, but she was determined not to let him see her emotions because he would continue to think of her as weak. "He means everything to his family, and I gave him back to them." She stood straighter, not realizing those words had been bottled up inside her. Her father put his fork down and although his expression remained closed, he looked at her in silence.

"I demand that you treat me with respect and respect my career choice because it's not going away, ever. I'm not a corporate type, I'm not going to be a university professor, and I'm never going to enter the business other than in a peripheral manner, Father. It's well past time you accept who I am." She paused and looked at the faces around the table, all of whom stared at her with rapt attention. Having been accepted by the group at the clinic based on her personality, her skills and a little coffee, it had given her the courage to stand up to her father. Being accepted by her peers was something she hadn't realized she'd needed until she had it. Now she was never going to let go of it.

"Who exactly are you?" Charles asked, his tone serious, all sarcasm gone.

"I am a nurse. I will always be a nurse and this clinic is a very important part of our community." She sucked in another breath and held her father's gaze, although she spoke to them all. "And when the time comes, all of you are going to cough up a healthy donation to keep it going."

"I see." He rested his elbows on the table and tented his fingers. That was always a bad sign. She knew it and sat down, still determined to hold her position. Charles was a businessman and a master manipulator, and she needed to be on her guard. "When will that time be?"

"I'm not sure yet, but soon. I've made the suggestion to put together a big fundraiser, and I've a preliminary plan, but Miguel is still working his numbers, too. The city was supposed to come through with additional funding, but they haven't." That was unfortunate for all of them.

"Who's been managing the money until now?" Arnold asked. He was the brother who made magic with numbers.

"Miguel has been doing everything, but it's simply too overwhelming for one person to be the director, the physician, the accountant and find more funding all at once."

"Well, Victoria, when you get the benefit together, you can count on me for assistance." Charles watched her.

Surprise and shock raced through her system, but at the same time a self-protective suspicion. "What are you playing at, Daddy? I'm not talking about loose change here. This clinic is a very worthy cause, and Miguel simply can't do it all by himself any longer. No one can." The light in him was rapidly burning out, and she was determined to help keep it going.

"I'll kick in some accounting help," her eldest brother, Arnold, said, and speared a bit of meat. "Set up a non-profit or something for him."

"Me, too!" Jessica, her niece of ten, said. "My class has raised money before, and we can help, too."

Tears that she'd held back now gushed forth, and Vicky allowed them to roll down her cheeks. "Thank you, Jessy." She looked at her father, afraid to hope that he was really seeing her for the first time, acknowledging her as an independent adult with a life and agenda of her own. “Are you really serious or are you just amusing yourself at my expense?”

“I’m certain it will be at *my* expense,” he said, and dropped his gaze with a clearing of his throat. “I’d forgotten what heart you have, Victoria, the passion you have for helping others. Please accept my apology and count on me to help out the clinic in any way I can.”

Victoria leaned her elbows on the table and tented her fingers this time, while holding her father’s gaze. “How about unrestricted access to your contact list?”

He roared in laughter and nearly tipped his chair over. “You are definitely my daughter!”

“I hope that’s a compliment,” she said as the family laughed, too.

“It is, Victoria, it is.” He reached across the table and squeezed her hand, then picked up his fork. “Now, tell me what kind of ideas you have and how the rest of us can help you. Of course we’ll provide the wine. Won’t do to have a Sterling-Thorne fundraiser without the family label.”

Victoria’s appetite returned with gusto as she outlined the ideas she had for the fundraiser. Everyone engaged in a vigorous discussion, tossing out ideas and hashing them over until a brilliant plan emerged that Vicky was certain would work.

Now all she had to do was convince Miguel.

Between extra duties at the clinic and checking on Carlos, there was simply little time to spare to talk to Miguel until the end of the week. He was as personable with the patients as he had always been, but now he’d clearly withdrawn into some sort of bubble that protected him from everything and everyone else. He was simply burned-out.

She lingered after the staff left, hoping to catch him, to talk to him. She approached his office, where he was spending more and more time, and had raised her hand to knock when his office phone rang. Easing away, she didn't want to eavesdrop and waited a few minutes until she heard him hang up.

"Miguel?" she called, and knocked on the door. "Got a few minutes?"

"Sure. Come in."

Vicky entered the office and nearly gasped. He looked terrible in the fluorescent lighting overhead. "You're not sleeping, are you?"

Before answering, he rubbed his face with his hands, as if trying to wake up, though it was the end of the day. "Is that what you wanted to talk about, my sleeping habits?"

"No, of course not, but—"

"What did you want?"

Taken aback by the gruff tone of his voice, she frowned, trying to decide what to do. "I wanted to talk to you about the fundraiser. I've got some ideas and can get moving on things now that we know Carlos is going to get better." She sighed. "That's at least one less thing to worry about now."

"Yeah, it is. I hadn't expected him to do so well so quickly."

"I'm just glad he is. The resilience of the young, you know?" She cleared her throat. "However, the problem for the clinic remains."

"The clinic problems have changed since we last talked. It may have to close."

"What?" That was something she'd never expected to hear. "Why?"

"I've been offered a job at the hospital in the trauma unit. And I've spent the last week on the phone trying to find someone to take over the clinic, but no one wants to do what I do and there simply isn't the funding to hire more staff." He angrily got to his feet and cursed under his breath. "Until I laid it all out on paper, I hadn't realized how well we did with so little help. No one is going to do what I've done. No one!" He threaded his fingers in his hair and groaned aloud. "If I want a life I have to close the clinic. What choice is that?"

"Miguel, be straight with me. What's going on?"

"I either have to sacrifice the clinic and the community if I want to take the university job or I have to sacrifice my life to keep this clinic going. This isn't what I set out to do when I took over the clinic."

"You've done a marvelous job with so many things here. Tilly told me how you turned it around in just over a year. That's astonishing."

"Yeah, by working my ass off." He turned to face her. "Do you know I haven't had a true vacation in three years, nearly four? There are so many family events that I've missed because of some crisis or another." Anger snapped in his dark eyes, and she knew it was focused on himself.

"That's not good, Miguel." She shook her head. "No one should sacrifice all their time like that. You deserve to have a life, too."

"Do I really?" he turned away from her and swore again. "I don't know if I deserve anything."

"That's not true. You've put your heart and your blood into this place."

"My brother's blood, you mean."

"What are you talking about?" That didn't make sense.

"Never mind. I'll just have to decline the job offer and carry on as usual."

"You can't mean that," she said. "I saw you in the trauma unit with Carlos and when he was injured. You were at your best, weren't you?"

"No." He shook his head in denial, but she knew the truth of it.

"Yes, you were. I've been around enough to know when a physician is truly in his element, when he knows what he is doing and what feeds his soul. That was it for you, Miguel. I saw it. I saw you."

"It was one incident."

"But it changed you, didn't it?"

"No. It merely pointed out all my failings."

"How can you say that? Carlos would be dead if it weren't for you."

"It doesn't matter."

"It does matter. His family sure as hell thinks it matters." She approached him and invaded his personal space. She closed in on him and tried to ease his pain. Carefully, she placed her hand on his forearm and squeezed. The muscles beneath her hand bunched and trembled, but she refused to release him. "Tell me what's bugging you."

"There's nothing to tell."

"That is an outright lie. Tell me." The gaze that met hers was devoid of life, of the passion she knew lived in him. She'd felt it, touched it, tasted it. "I'm not going anywhere until you talk to me."

"Vicky, it's none of your business. It's history, my history, and—"

"It's eating you alive," she whispered. Never in her life had she assaulted a man, but she was about to if he didn't start talking. Some sort of fearlessness came over her, and she placed her arms around his shoulders to bring him closer. His body was stiff and resisting.

Miguel clamped his hands around her wrists, intending to drag her arms away, but he didn't. Something about the way she moved, the way she smelled, the way she felt so close to him stopped him. Then he looked into her eyes, and he was done for.

"Vicky." His voice was a hoarse whisper. "Vicky."

"It's okay, Miguel. It's okay. I'm here for you."

He didn't know if things would ever be okay again, and right now he didn't care. Instead of putting her away from him, he grabbed her tight against him. Emotions and feelings that he'd kept locked up inside of him burst free. Right now, talking wasn't what he wanted.

He pulled back, cupped both hands around Vicky's face and kissed her. Hard and hungry, he wanted her. There was no hesitation in her response as she parted her lips to his tongue. Each stroke of her silky tongue met his and he put all of the pain, the emotion of his past into the kiss. With her arms linked tight around his neck, he pressed one hand to her back and allowed the other to drift down to that lovely backside he'd noticed the first day. He cupped one hand against her curved bottom and then brought the other hand down. Somehow he managed to move so that he pressed her against the wall. A groan of pure lust rumbled deep in his chest. If he didn't control himself right now, he might commit an act he'd likely regret.

Easing back, he gave her a little room, but didn't let go of her. She was a beauty inside and out, and he'd been an idiot for not seeing it. Although he wanted her, he didn't belong in her life any more than she belonged in his. They either needed to end this little flirtation of theirs or take it all the way and be done with it. As he looked at her flushed cheeks and the way her eyes went soft, the ruby lips, he doubted that making love to her for one night would ever be enough. If he jumped into that water, he'd certainly drown.

"Can you talk now?" she asked, and cupped her hand against his cheek. "I don't mean to pry into your life, but something's almost destroying you, and it might help to talk about it."

Easing back some more, he considered her words. "Nothing can help this." He'd never really tried, but the pain ran so deep, he couldn't conceive of anything ever releasing it. It was part of him.

"Tell me." She took his hand, led him out of the office and locked the door to the clinic. She made a pot of coffee and pulled out a packet of crackers and a jar of peanut butter from the cupboard. After things were ready, they sat on the floor of the waiting area.

"You really don't know what you're letting yourself in for," he said, trying to make light of the situation, but he also recognized the wisdom of her words. Who knew? Maybe something could help. If anyone could make it happen, he knew it would be Vicky.

"Just start talking. I know you were awfully worried about Carlos and rightfully so, but after he started to improve, you didn't."

Miguel closed his eyes and let the emotions of that day wash over him. Images of his brother and Carlos meshed together and blended until they nearly became one. "The incident with Carlos was nearly a replay of the night my brother, Emilio, died." Inside him a tremor started. His hand shook as he reached for a cracker.

"Miguel, I didn't know."

"I know." He patted her shoulder and tried not to fall too far into those blue eyes of hers. "You couldn't have. Carlos, of course, is Carlos, but he looks nearly identical to my brother."

Vicky's eyes widened. She knew the implications. "That brought it all back again, didn't it? I'd guess that's a case of PTSD you didn't expect."

"Yeah. It was like reliving it all over again, except that this time you were there, and Carlos survived." He huffed out a sigh filled with regrets he could never change. "Emilio died on the sidewalk in my arms. I had to tell my family that he'd been shot by the gang I'd been trying to get him away from." The irony of it hadn't eluded him.

"Oh, my God, Miguel. You've kept this inside until now?"

"I took responsibility for what was my fault." It was that simple to him. He was older, he was the responsible one.

"How could any of it be your fault? The gang pulled the trigger."

"I might as well have. I was trying to persuade the gang leader, Juan, to leave Emilio alone, and he was about to shoot me. Emilio dived in and took the bullet that was meant for me."

Tears filled her eyes as she watched him tell the story and she waited until he was finished speaking to ask questions. "How old were you when this happened?"

"Twenty-one. I was the oldest, responsible." He held up his wrist and pointed out the silver bracelet he wore. "I'd just finished college, was home on break before medical school. This was a present for Emilio, but I never got to give it to him."

"I've noticed it. It's beautiful."

"It reminds me every day of how I failed my family and my brother, that I was responsible for his death." He'd never taken it off.

"Where is this Juan now?"

"In jail. For another murder." He snorted in disgust. "At least they got him for that one."

"I'd say he's where he belongs, and so are you." She placed her hand over his. "Nothing you've told me changes the fact that you are doing very good things for your community. And no part of Emilio's death was your fault. You've got to know that."

"If I hadn't tried to get him out, he might be alive now."

"Or he might not. He could have been killed in another incident. You'll never know. But you have to let him go, Miguel. That's the only way you'll be free. You've been punishing yourself with this clinic, and now I know why. You think if you work yourself to death by saving others, it will pay for your crime, but it wasn't yours to pay for."

He looked at her and opened his mouth to deny everything, but he couldn't. The words just wouldn't come. Instead, he needed a change of pace. "Tell me what you have in mind for the fundraiser, and I'll tell you what I think."

"Change of topic won't get you off the hook," she said, but opened a folder filled with a lot of papers and numbers. "'A Night for a Life' is the tentative title I've given the event. If people spend one night bringing in money to the clinic, it will save a life." She paused and looked at him. "If we do this right, the clinic will run itself. My brother can set up the nonprofit part of it, and you'll have the freedom and the time to work at the hospital, too."

Fascinated, he listened to her give the minipresentation. No fancy computer programs, just a simple retelling of her plan for funding the clinic, for helping him to achieve his dream of returning to the trauma unit and keeping the clinic alive, as well.

He'd been so wrong about Vicky Sterling-Thorne.

CHAPTER FOURTEEN

MIGUEL lay in bed sleepless, restless, his mind racing as midnight approached. Spring eased its way into summer with bright beautiful days and evenings that were designed for sleeping with the windows open to catch any stray breeze that happened by. This was the beauty of living in the high desert: warm days, balmy nights.

Another week had passed, seeing Carlos's continued improvement. At least that was one worry off his mind. The days were full of patients and the evenings full of fundraising plans. Now that he was on board with the idea, he was really enjoying the process of putting together such an event. It was a far cry from the bake sales and car washes he'd envisioned. He and Vicky worked together, tirelessly caring for patients and planning for the event. In doing so, he was seeing her in a different light that was not as unflattering as he'd thought in the beginning. Now he had no regrets that he'd hired her.

He'd come to depend on her more than he'd ever thought he could and the ice surrounding his heart had begun to melt because of her. That was another thing he never thought he'd experience. She brought new life to the clinic and was slowly bringing new life to him.

The red numbers on the bedside clock showed it was

midnight. Frustrated, he sat up and shook off the sheet. Before he knew it the phone was in his hand and he'd dialed Vicky's number. If she didn't answer in the first ring or two he'd hang up, but he just wanted to talk to her. Just had to hear her voice. Now.

"Hello?"

Miguel nearly dropped to his knees at the husky, sexy tone of her voice. "It's Miguel. Did I wake you?" He could just imagine her all rumpled with sleep, soft and sexy, as she reached for the phone in the dark.

"Sort of. I was resting but not really asleep. You know that in-between state?"

"I know it." He'd been in it.

"What's up besides us?"

He smiled at that. One of the things he'd come to love about her was the subtle sense of humour she had. The patients responded to it, and he found himself responding, as well. "I…I don't know. I just wanted to talk to you for a minute."

"Restless, huh? Usually when I'm restless a walk helps settle me down."

"A walk at midnight?" He'd never thought of that.

"Definitely. Why don't you come over, and I'll take you for a midnight stroll like you've never imagined."

Intriguing. "I'll get dressed."

"Me, too." She gave him her address and they hung up. Adrenaline and anticipation replaced the restlessness than ran through his veins. He didn't know what kind of midnight walk she had in mind, but anything had to be better than the current situation he was in.

In short order he made the trip to her home in the north valley area of Albuquerque. Though not far away in distance, the area was far away, a throwback, in time.

Huge trees and mature foliage hugged both sides of the road mixed with open fields for alfalfa and grazing horses. She lived in a caretaker's cottage in the middle of the vineyard, she had said. Someday he'd like to see this area during daylight. As beautiful as it was at night, he wanted to see it in the light of day. He made the turn onto a narrow lane, darkened by the dense cottonwood trees overhead. It almost put him in another land or era. No wonder she loved it here.

The porch light guided him and in minutes he saw her standing by the front door of a quaint cottage nearly enveloped with dark ivy and surrounded by rose bushes. He'd never seen her looking so casual, in a plain shirt, denim shorts and flimsy sandals. He'd never seen her looking so luscious, either. This was definitely where he wanted to be instead of rolling around in his bed.

"Made it okay?" she asked as he stepped out of the truck.

"No problem. Love that GPS."

With a sideways smile and eyes full of mystery, she held out her hand. "Let's walk." She led the way into the incredibly dark night, as if she'd taken this path many times. With only a tiny flashlight in her hand that hardly lent illumination, he followed her. Out here there were no streetlights. They were surrounded by acres and acres of vineyard and brilliant galaxies overhead.

In silence they strolled as the sounds of the night rose up around them. Crickets chimed their rhythmic songs, cicadas buzzed in the trees overhead, a delightful breeze stroked his skin, and he began to relax. The stress of the past two weeks was beginning to fade with the feel of her soft hand in his.

He took a deep breath, catching the fragrances of

the night. Fresh dirt, the sweet scent of honeysuckle and Spanish broom bushes that had to be nearby. He'd know those scents anywhere. Large, lush leaves of the grapevines brushed his arms and legs, the foliage reaching out from the strength of the main vines.

"This is very nice."

"*Nice?* This is awesome." She gave his hand a squeeze. "I love this walk. There are times I just can't sleep and a stroll through the vines helps me to relax. You can't see it now, but over there is the river." She paused and pointed to the west. The unmistakable snort of a horse made him smile.

"I think we're disturbing someone's sleep."

"They'll get over it." They kept walking.

He was glad she had his hand or he would have been lost for certain. As they rounded a bend in the path, the glint of moonlight off the river caught his eye. The thought of her half-naked and wet was enough to set his imagine on fire. Right now, with her in the middle of the night, he wanted to set his imagination free. He wanted to stop and savor the night and everything it had to offer.

"You ever swim down here?"

"Not in the river. Too unpredictable for me." She tugged on his hand. "But there's a pool at the main house. We can slip in for a quick dip."

"If it's a bad idea, I'll understand." But the thought of getting her alone and naked and wet was more than he could resist.

"It's a great idea. My father's not home right now, but he won't mind, anyway."

Clenching his jaw, as a wave of desire hit him, he stopped there. Having a tryst in the middle of the night was something he'd have done in his younger days, but now having one with his coworker wasn't on the agenda. Things would never be the same between them, and he wasn't willing to ruin his relationship with Vicky just for sex. He'd have to reel in his libido as long as he continued to work with her. Once he left the clinic, things might be different, but there was no guarantee in that. "As much as I'd like to, I don't think we should."

"Why not? It's not like we'll be naked or anything."

"We won't?" That stopped him. "Uh, why not?"

She giggled. "Because I'll put on my swimsuit and you can borrow a pair of my brother's trunks, that's why. They're clean."

"Oh." So much for libido and a wet, naked woman.

She laughed again. "You sound so disappointed."

"I am." But he laughed and the feeling swirling inside his chest was a good one. One he hadn't let himself experience in way too long. "Maybe a cool swim is just what I need after all."

"Right this way."

Miguel changed first and eased into the pool. Submerging himself fully, he allowed the water to wash over him. This was a luxury he'd never imagined. He pushed off the bottom and swam as far as he could in one breath, then surfaced for air. Just as he came up, Vicky launched herself from the diving board. Though there were lights at the bottom of the pool, she hadn't seen him, and he couldn't get out of the way fast enough. He submerged beneath her and came up just inches away.

"Miguel! I didn't see you. Are you okay?" She

reached out and placed her hands on his shoulders as they trod water.

It didn't matter what he told himself before and even if she wasn't naked, she was certainly wet and luscious in a barely-there bikini, and he wanted her. With one arm he snagged her around the waist and brought her fully against him, dragging her to the side of the pool. Now that the restraints had been loosened, he allowed himself to look down at her, to take in all that she was and enjoy his gaze wander over her. "I'm just fine." With her clinging to him, he approached the side of the pool where he could put his feet on the bottom.

Before he even knew what he was doing, he kissed her. Nothing was going to stop him from feeling every inch of her against him. He pressed her tight and the backs of his hands protected her delicate skin from rubbing against the side.

Slowly and deeply he took her, his lips, his mouth, his tongue, every breath he took seeming to become part of her. There was magic in the night and magic going on between them. The low groan in her throat made his desire flare higher and his arousal was both pleasurable and painful. He wanted her and as she raised her legs to wrap them around his hips, there was no doubt that she wanted him, too.

Lifting one hand, he slipped a thumb beneath the flimsy bikini top that clung to her skin and cupped her breast. The weight of her, the tight nipple in his hand felt so right. He wanted all of her filling his hands, filling his senses, and he tugged on the string that held the top together. In seconds it floated away to the bottom of the pool, like a leaf to the bottom of the river.

Dragging his mouth away from hers, he licked his

way down her neck and over one collarbone. Scooping a nipple into his mouth, he suckled hard, stroking the tight flesh with his tongue, wanting to send her as far into the abyss as he already was.

Vicky had never felt as alive, as filled with desire as she was at this moment. The water licked her skin, adding to the delicious sensation of Miguel teasing her nipple. Her senses were on overload and there was only one way to fix it. Pulling his head up, she spread kisses over his neck, his face, his eyes, and settled on his mouth for a long slow drink. Groaning, he pressed her against the edge of the pool again and his arousal burned into her. She wanted him as she'd never wanted any man in her life. She'd never been a great judge of men, but in Miguel there was a hidden heart of gold. Somehow she knew it.

"Let's go to the cottage." She stroked her hand down his face and let it rest on his chest. "We need to get out of these wet clothes."

He dug his fingers into her hips, everything about him intense and aroused. Even in the dim lighting from around the pool she saw the desire burning in his eyes. She wanted him, too. There was nothing to hold either of them back. Any nagging doubts had faded away.

"I want that very much, but if we make love it will change everything between us." He took in a deep breath and held her gaze. "Not just some things. Everything."

"I think things have already changed between us. We've been circling this moment since we met." Feeling bolder than she ever had, she brought his hand back to her breast, loving the feel of his skin sliding against hers, needing to feel the vitality he infused into her with his touch. This was the way things were supposed to be between a man and a woman. This was the way it was supposed to feel, and she didn't want to let it go. "I want things to change between us, Miguel." She stroked his face again, loving the textures of him against her. "I want to make love to you."

Groaning, he hugged her close, then pressed her against the side again. He trembled in her arms. As she moved, he winced then pulled back.

"What is it?"

Cupping her face, he pressed a kiss to her mouth and eased her toward the steps. "I think the cement is chipped. Just scraped my hand on the side, but it's nothing."

Vicky pulled back. "Let me see. Doctors are the worst patients, you know."

"Seriously, it's just a scratch." He turned his hand over to show her, and she gasped at the blood streaming from several small wounds. "This isn't nothing." She looked back at the pool and saw the broken and chipped spot that she had avoided every time she swam lately. "Dammit. Daddy was supposed to have had that fixed by now." She grabbed a towel and wrapped it around her. Her breath came out in panting gasps as she stood trembling beside him. "Why don't we go get that fixed?" She held out her hand to him.

He took it and they returned to the cottage. With the towel knotted in the front, Vicky tended to the abrasions that were really nothing, but he enjoyed the touch of her and the way she fussed over him.

With the gentle touch that he had seen her use countless times on patients in the clinic, she tended to the small cuts as if they were the most urgent of injuries.

That made him smile inside and the warmth of love pulsed out with each beat of his heart.

Unexpected moisture filled his eyes and the warmth began to burn in his lungs. He couldn't do it. He couldn't have a night of passion with Vicky and walk away from her. But he couldn't give her what she needed and what she deserved either.

Curling his hands into fists, he pulled away from her. He had to end it now, no matter how much it hurt him.

Vicky stared up at him, her eyes brimming with tears. "Miguel?" Her breath came in short gasps. "You're leaving, aren't you?"

The pain squeezed his throat shut. Though he opened his mouth, he couldn't speak. He'd never experienced such anguish tearing him apart. "I...have to."

"No, you don't. We can just talk or sleep."

A vulgar laugh opened his throat. "If I stayed, we wouldn't be sleeping."

"I can live with a sleepless night, Miguel." She took a step closer and some of the tears fell from her eyes. "I don't want to spend a sleepless night without you beside me."

"Vicky, you deserve so much better, so much more than what I can give you." He backed up and spun around in a circle. "I mean, just look at what you're used to. This is so far away from what I come from, from who I am, it might as well be the other side of the world."

"I don't need this! I don't want this." She moved closer to him. "The outer shell of this life has cost me more than you'll ever know." Tears flowed as anger snapped in her eyes. "Existing in this environment isn't living. I've only begun to live, to grow, to love since I started at the clinic." She sucked in a ragged breath. "I want more of it. I *need* more of it. Of you."

"Vicky," he said, and his voice cracked. The emotion in the room nearly sizzled between them. "I'm broken inside. Whatever capacity I had to love another died a long time ago."

"That's not true. I saw you with your family, with Carlos's family. There was love and compassion in you then. It's not gone, it's just been in hiding for a long time."

"I'm sorry. If I were different, maybe things could have worked between us."

"If I wanted somebody different, I could have had them."

"I'm sorry." He cupped his hands around her face and pulled her close for one last hard kiss before he walked away from her forever.

CHAPTER FIFTEEN

VICKY sobbed the remainder of the night into her pillow. Around dawn she slept, but only for a few elusive hours. Erotic dreams of Miguel beside her melded into the nightmare of reality. Her life was destined for failure. If she'd hidden her identity from Miguel he'd have been furious when he'd found out. Not hiding her identity had turned out just as bad. Either way, her family name interfered with her ability to have a normal life and she was damned sick of it.

They still had to get through the next week together. The fundraiser was on Saturday night, and she didn't know how either of them would survive the week working together. After that she would turn in her resignation. There was no point in staying at the clinic. She had proved to her father and to herself that she could work in that environment. Maybe she would go to University Hospital, too. They were always looking for nurses and she'd be able to hide more easily among a larger staff.

Tears filled her eyes as she thought of leaving those patients and the staff she'd come to love. On Monday she would have to face Miguel again, and she didn't know how she was going to do that without breaking down and breaking her heart.

* * *

Monday morning arrived and Vicky strolled through the doors a few minutes early. After putting on the first pot of coffee, she chatted with Tilly and the other staff members who arrived in the minutes before Miguel. Trying to appear normal took a monumental effort.

There was a break in his stride as he came through the door and saw her, then he continued on to his office.

As always, Mondays were the busiest of days and the flow of patients didn't let up until noon. Miguel caught her eye as she was about to enter the staff room for a much-needed break. With a nod, he turned and headed to his office. She followed, not sure what was going to happen but she was determined to see it through. She was a Sterling-Thorne after all, and they were made of tough stuff.

She shut the door and stood inside his office, just across the desk from the man who had held her in his arms only two nights ago. "Did you need something?" she asked.

"I didn't expect to see you this morning." There was no warmth in his gaze, just cold indifference. Somehow that was worse than his anger.

"Why not? Just because we had a philosophical difference on a personal level, it doesn't mean I quit my job."

"It would be easier if you did."

She smiled at that. "I know it would, but I'm done making things easier on people. I'm doing what's right for me. I love this job and these people that I work with, the staff as well as the patients." She huffed out a breath and realized that every word of it was true. She wasn't going anywhere. "If you don't want me to work here any more, you're going to have to fire me and then *you* get to tell everyone." Without waiting for his reaction, she left the office.

The trembling began in her arms and wound its way around to her stomach then down her legs. If she didn't sit soon, she was going to fall over. The conviction of her words surprised her, but as she'd told Miguel, she'd realized they were true. She turned down a hallway that led to a side door. She had to get outside for a breath of fresh air, just for a minute, then she'd head back inside and back to work.

Just as she opened the door, excited screams rang out behind her. "What in the world...?" she mumbled. The clinic closed for lunch, so there weren't any patients present at the moment. What could be going on? Reluctantly, she returned to the staff lounge and discovered people laughing and crying at the same time. They were grouped so that she couldn't see what they were looking at.

"Vicky?" Carlos called to her.

"Carlos!" She found herself enveloped in the young man's hug. "What are you doing here?" The joy at his recovery pushed away the sad feelings in her heart.

Too many emotions crowded around in her and tears fell from her eyes as she pressed her hands to her cheeks. But they were good tears, and she let them go. Hiding her emotions had never gotten her anything, so why waste the energy?

"I'm back for a visit. I go to therapy nearby, so I wanted to stop and see if anyone had missed me." He grinned and the room exploded in relieved laughter. Good wishes and gentle pats on the back were exchanged.

When Vicky looked up, Miguel stood across the

room, his dark eyes intent on her for a second, then he looked at Carlos and his expression changed. In just a few steps he had crossed the room and enveloped the young man in his arms. "Why didn't you tell us you were coming?"

"That takes the surprise out of it," he said. They spoke in an excited mix of English and Spanish and Vicky could follow some of it, but it was obvious that everyone was glad to see Carlos upright and looking so well. Though he looked fit enough, there was a slight sheen of perspiration on his forehead and he hadn't quite lost his hospital pallor.

He placed a hand on the back of a chair, and Vicky noticed that it trembled.

"Sit down, why don't you?" She gestured for him to sit and took a chair herself, knowing that he'd never admit to feeling weak among his friends. Machismo ran deep in him, and he wasn't about to give it up now. "We were just about to have lunch. Did you want to join us?"

"Sure. Catch me up on what's going on around here. When's the fundraiser?" He looked across the small table at Miguel for the answer.

"We're going to have to cancel the event." He looked away and pressed his lips together.

A gasp rose in the room and worried glances were exchanged.

"No, we're not. The fundraiser is on Saturday night." Vicky focused on Miguel. What was he doing? "The clinic needs this."

"I've reconsidered. I won't leave. We'll just go on the way we were before."

"Leave? What are you talking about?" Confused, Carlos looked between the two. "What's going on?"

"Miguel's been offered a position at the trauma unit at University Hospital."

"That's great, man," he said, then frowned. "Oh, but not great for us, though."

"Exactly. Which is why I'm going to decline the offer. I can't walk away from everyone here."

She looked at Miguel and knew she loved him. "Don't make me do it, Miguel."

Now it was his turn to be confused. "Do what?"

She spoke to Carlos and the rest of the staff. "It's his dream to work in the trauma unit again. He was in his element when you were injured, and I've never seen him work better, though he's much too modest to admit that out loud. As much as he loves this place, his talent is wasted here."

"Vicky—"

Carlos simply looked at Miguel. "You have to, M. You saved my life and if you can save other people too, you have to do it."

"I'm not leaving here. I've made a commitment to the people in this community."

"And you won't be breaking it by going to the hospital," Vicky said.

Staff members stood up and gathered around the table, each of them placing a hand of encouragement on Miguel. Good wishes and words of luck rang throughout the room.

He cleared his throat and looked down. Tears welled in Vicky's eyes at the emotion he struggled to hide. He loved these people, and they loved him right back. He'd never be far from them, far from this place where his heart lived, but his dreams weren't going to wait. She was sure of it.

The day seemed to struggle forward as much as Vicky did. It was one of those painful afternoons where she worked hard to put one foot in front of the other and each movement was a chore.

Finally, all of the patients were seen and the clinic had been put to rights for the next morning. A yawn surprised her, and she covered it with her hand.

"Worn-out, are you?" Tilly asked as she gathered her things.

"Definitely."

"You and Miguel have been working your tails off to get things ready for Saturday night while working all day long." She shook her head in amazement. "Good thing you two are young."

They chatted another minute or two as the other staff filed out. "It will be good when it's over, though. The clinic will be its own nonprofit organization and it will be able to almost run itself. Miguel will be able to take the new position and everyone will be happy." She sighed as she thought about it. His work and his presence here would never be forgotten, she was certain of it.

"What about you?" Tilly asked.

"What about me?"

"You mentioned the clinic and Miguel, but not what you're going to do after it's all over. Will you still stay?"

For a second or two she thought about it. What was she going to do? She'd changed since she'd first arrived. "I'll be back on Monday, like the rest of you, ready for another round of taking care of people." She hugged the smaller woman's shoulders with one arm. "It's what people like you and me do, Tilly. We take care of people, right?"

Tilly patted her hand. "Right. See you in the morning."

Could it really be that simple? Miguel hadn't meant to listen in on the earlier conversation between Tilly and Vicky at the clinic, but he had. He arrived home and paused inside the door as emotions he'd held at bay now slammed into him. The sentiment in Vicky's voice was so sure, so filled with conviction that he wanted to believe in her in the same way that she believed in him.

Shoving his hands into his hair, he curled his fingers, pulling his hair until it hurt. He didn't know what to do. Giving in to the passion he felt for Vicky would be so very easy, but with nothing to offer her, nothing she didn't already have, how could he pursue her? Lying to himself would only get both of them into trouble and hurt Vicky more than he already had. Lies. They were what always got people into trouble, and he'd never tolerated them. Lies were what had gotten his brother killed.

He closed his eyes and images of his brother's death hit him, opened up the wound and let the pain flow. He'd never gotten over it, he knew. Family events, the look in people's eyes, the hugs that seemed to go on forever all came back now to torture him. That was why he'd wanted Vicky at the party with him, to provide a buffer between his family and himself. That hadn't turned out the way he'd planned. That had only given him the opportunity to fall in love with a woman he could never have.

The voice he hadn't heard in a decade whispered into the room and enveloped him in a swirl of warm comfort.

It wasn't your fault. It wasn't your fault, brother.

The pain in Miguel's heart felt as if he would die from it and his breath ceased. If he had been shot with an arrow, his heart couldn't have hurt any less. Tears that he'd held back for so many years filled his eyes, and he gasped for breath.

Let go, brother, just let me go.

He looked down at the bracelet on his right wrist and blinked to clear his vision. The bracelet had been there as a symbol to himself, and everyone who knew him, of his guilt, his chain to the past. He'd never taken it off. Not since that night so long ago. The metal that had always burned hot against his skin now cooled, the heat leaving it.

With the echo of Emilio's voice ringing in his ears, he moved down the hallway to the pictures and stopped in front of one of his brother. Memories of their childhood flashed through him. He placed the fingers of his left hand over the warm silver and pulled off the bracelet. As he stared at the photograph, the pain in his chest began to ease, replaced with a warm pulse he hadn't felt for a long time. He hung the bracelet on a corner of the picture frame.

He didn't need it any longer.

CHAPTER SIXTEEN

VICKY had taken a room at the hotel for the night, as had been her custom for every fundraiser she'd ever attended. If she needed a break from the party she could go to her room, and when she was through for the night it was simpler to take the elevator than to try to negotiate driving in a fancy gown and flimsy shoes.

She'd made the final arrangements this evening then spent some time preparing herself. There were so many people that she'd see tonight that she had to have her Victoria face on for. That took preparation of a certain kind. And since the evening was for Miguel's clinic, he and her father were certain to meet. There were a few key introductions that she wanted to make to Miguel that could help with the future of the clinic, too.

That was anxiety of a completely different sort.

Whether Miguel would be warm or cool tonight, she had no idea. Either way, he'd see the woman behind the name tonight. So far she'd always been Vicky to him. Tonight Victoria would be on display. Tonight would reveal whether they truly had a chance to work things out. If he could accept who she was, that was one thing. If he couldn't, then things were well and truly over between them.

She stuck a few items plus the key card into a tiny purse that matched her dress and inspected herself in the mirror. The dress was another of her brother's creations and as usual he'd spared her no extra fabric.

After a calming breath, she turned on a dim light by the bed, then left the room to see what fate had in store for her in the ballroom.

The tux was too tight. And who in their right minds had invented the cummerbund? Dress shoes looked good, but other than that they were a waste, too. No wonder women had a love-hate relationship with high heels.

Miguel stood in the men's room, which was nearly as big as his entire bungalow. Looking in the mirror, he adjusted his tie a bit to the left then to the right. Right back where it wanted to go anyway. He'd arrived early to help Vicky with any final arrangements, but she had apparently already come and gone, leaving him with more minutes to spare than he cared to have. A stroll around the lush gardens killed a few minutes, but the nervousness and anxiety boiling inside him wouldn't be quieted so easily.

So many things were riding on the success of this night and any number of things could go wrong.

Maybe a quick trip to the bar would calm his nerves. He reentered the hallway, and his shoes made crisp sounds on the tile flooring.

"Dr. Torres!" A familiar woman's voice called to him. A smile seemed to grow from his chest and made its way to his face. Carlos and his parents had entered and his mother waved.

He greeted them and gave a peck on the cheek to

Priscilla. "You know you don't have to call me Doctor. You're family."

"Oh, not on a night like this," she said, wide-eyed. "This is your night, *mijo,* and you deserve all the respect that comes to you." She looked up at her son with such affection and love that a lump formed in Miguel's throat. "You saved my son and there is nothing I won't do for you."

He shook Carlos's hand. "You're looking fit. How do you feel?"

"Great." He stuck a finger in his collar. "Tux is a little tight, but I'll live."

"Bah. Tight. He's lost twenty pounds since he was injured, and I think I've found them all!" Priscilla gave a laugh and patted her stomach.

"There will be plenty for him to eat tonight."

After that the guests began to arrive in earnest. People that he knew from the clinic and others he recognized from the community. Other people he didn't know but had to be among the wealthiest people he'd ever seen.

When a man in his mid-thirties entered the lobby with two clinging women dressed in haute couture, he hid a grin. That had to be the fashion-designer brother of Vicky's.

The entire group stopped in front of him and the man gave Miguel the once-over with his eyes. "You must be the doctor," he said, and held out his hand.

"I must be or I'm at the wrong party." Miguel shook the man's hand, liking him immediately.

"I'm Edward, Victoria's brother." One of the tall women with Edward gave a dramatic sigh.

"Quite the group you have here," Miguel said.

"Yes, isn't it?" Edward sported a woman on each arm. "I couldn't decide who to bring, so I brought both."

"Why limit yourself?" He grinned.

"Indeed. Do you know where Victoria is?"

"I haven't seen her, but she should be here somewhere."

"Ladies, shall we go and see what sort of entertainment awaits us?" Without waiting for an answer, Edward strode forward and Miguel followed the small group.

"I'll catch you later," Carlos said, and walked beside Miguel. "Hey, what's with this 'Victoria' stuff? What's up with you and Vicky?"

Miguel paused inside the ballroom and pulled Carlos to the side. "Vicky…isn't who you think she is."

"What? What do you mean? You mean she's not a nurse?" His eyes went wide.

"Yes, she's a nurse—"

"Don't tell me she's a dude!"

"Carlos—"

"I saw that movie once, you know?" The man paled.

"No, just listen, will you?" He sighed, hating to break the news to Carlos. "She belongs to the family of Sterling-Thorne. She's Victoria Sterling-Thorne."

"Wow. You mean the wine people?" Carlos's eyes got very big at the mention of the name. He was obviously impressed.

"Exactly."

Carlos whistled. "I didn't know. I thought she was just a regular nurse. Way to go, man."

"What are you talking about?" Miguel frowned, not liking the implication of that.

"You hooking up with such a rich woman."

"Vicky and I aren't hooked up."

"Why not? You're perfect together."

"I don't think so." That comment was a small taste of what Vicky had been talking about, and this was coming from a trusted friend. Had he treated Vicky differently because he'd known who she was? He didn't know, but she had been right to be cautious.

Somehow something in the room changed, and he looked up. Scanning the crowd, he first saw a large group of people settling down at richly appointed tables, then his chest stopped moving and he couldn't draw breath.

Vicky stood across the room and stared at him. Just like in the movies, everything else faded away from his vision and he only saw her. Tall, lithe and elegant, she shimmered in the light. Sequins on the dress, patterned like an orchid, glinted with the slightest move she made. The dress hugged every curve and set her figure off magnificently. There were no sleeves, just small straps that disappeared against her skin.

Miguel was simply stunned stupid by the sight of her.

Someone placed a finger beneath his chin and pushed. "You look like a hound dog, man," Carlos said. "Try to look professional, will you?"

Right now, staring at Vicky, he felt like one. "I don't know what you mean." He blinked and with an effort faced the younger man.

"You look like you want to take a bite out of her."

"That's not true."

"Well, if you don't, I will." He straightened his tie and took a step toward Vicky.

"Oh, no, you don't. You're entirely too young."

"A man needs practice, right?"

Carlos was teasing him, and he played right along. "Go practice on someone else."

"I knew there was something going on between you two. From the first day, I knew it."

"There's nothing going on between us."

Carlos looked at Vicky, then back at him. "If there isn't, there should be." He nudged Miguel. "Go talk to her, you know you want to. Just don't drool on her dress."

"I'll try to be civil."

"Good. I'm gonna check out the food. I'll catch you later." After a quick rap of his knuckles against Miguel's, Carlos left him alone. Unable to delay any longer, he made his way across the dance floor to where Vicky stood greeting people. The closer he got to her, the thicker his tongue felt, and he didn't even know if he could speak.

"Victoria!" An older gentleman, tall and upright, leaned over and kissed her on the cheek. "It's wonderful to see you doing good things again." He released her and his wife embraced Vicky.

"Charity was your mother's life after you children. She would be so proud of you."

"Thank you, both." She turned to Miguel and he moved closer to her. That fragrance of hers sinuously invaded his mind and his heart, drawing him ever closer to her flame. "This is Dr. Miguel Torres, the medical director of the clinic. Dr. Torres, this is Mr. Thomas and and Mrs. Sally Hampton. They own the Hampton Inn chain."

"Pleasure to meet you," Miguel said, and he was

certainly impressed at how casually Vicky introduced them. She was in her element here.

"Outstanding work you're doing in your clinic, Dr. Torres. Outstanding." They shook hands. "We need more physicians like you, not more hospital conglomerations that take you away from your patients."

"Thank you. You sound as if you have some experience in that arena."

"I'm an old adman, but two of my sons chose medicine." He raised his eyes skyward. "The stories they tell are shocking."

"Thank you very much for supporting the clinic. It means a lot to everyone involved."

"My sons are out of state, but they have sent along their regards," Mr. Hampton said, and retrieved a long envelope from his jacket. "Along with a donation. They grew up here and have a great fondness for the work you do at ground level."

Miguel took the envelope and tucked it inside his tux, humbled at the generosity of strangers. "Please give them my greatest thanks, sir." He'd never expected such a generous outpouring for the clinic. Never. He looked at Vicky, who wore an enigmatic smile.

"Lovely to see you again. Save me a dance later," Vicky said. She took Miguel's arm and maneuvered them toward another couple.

"Nicely done." Large crowds weren't within his comfort zone, but Vicky looked like a professional.

"Years of practice." She shrugged off the compliment. "Actually, he's like an uncle to me. I've known him my whole life."

Another couple of equal standing in the community approached them. Introductions were made and the interaction was repeated dozens of times over the course of the next two hours. Vicky truly knew how to charm people and share her wit so that everyone knew she saw them and heard what they had to say. He received several more private envelopes for the clinic.

"Dr. Torres, this is Dr. Flemming, a physician who might be interested in taking a hands-on role at the clinic."

Surprise filled Miguel. "Pleasure," he said, and shook the older man's hand. "I'd love to have you come visit and see what we do."

"Absolutely. I'm heading toward part-time employment, but I'm not ready to retire all the way yet." He smiled and creases appeared around his eyes. "I'll call you next week and we'll set something up."

"I'll look forward to it." Excitement pulsed through him. There were possibilities in a meeting like that. And it was all thanks to Vicky. "Would you like something to drink?" he asked. After so much time spent talking, he was parched.

"Yes. Champagne would be lovely." She surveyed the room. "Looks like everyone is settling down to eat. This is usually the time I have a little refreshment."

"It would be a shame to let all of that fabulous food go to waste."

"Absolutely." They sat at a reserved table and were served immediately by the attentive waitstaff. The food was incredible, but Vicky seemed to be more attentive to the goings-on at other tables than to what was on her plate.

"Not hungry?"

She sipped her champagne. "I'm okay. At functions

like this my appetite usually spirals down to nothing. Too anxious to eat much."

"That's a shame. This is really good." He set his fork by his plate and took a closer look at her. She looked beautiful, her hair and makeup perfect, but beneath that she was pale and nervous. She'd hidden herself for so many years that she'd nearly fooled him. "What's really going on?"

The flash of her eyes down to her glass and then back at him told it all. This was the Victoria she'd talked about. And he understood it all. It wasn't just this event, it was every day of her life that wasn't at the clinic. This persona made it difficult to have a life that wasn't under a microscope all the time.

The part of him that had sworn not to empathize with her, to feel sorry for her seemed to have folded away with the feelings he'd had for his brother. The empty space that had held his pain was now slowly being filled with something else. Something unexpected and warm.

Without preamble, the music began. A medley of songs, old and new, faded away into a song that was certain to be an audience favorite. As Miguel watched, couples gathered on the dance floor. Many of them had obviously danced together for years. The way they moved together, flowed with each other, anticipating each move the other made, made it obvious.

This was a night like no other and he was realizing that Vicky was a woman like no other. When he left the clinic, he'd likely never see her again. Could he live with that? Could he walk away from her? Standing, he held out his hand to her, careful to keep his features controlled. This was not the time or place for any revelations, even if he had any. "Will you dance with me?" There was so much more than that one simple question.

The fatigue in her eyes lifted and a small smile tugged at the corners of her mouth. "I thought you'd never ask." She placed her hand in his and tonight it felt daintier, more fragile, than it ever had. That was an illusion, he knew, the same way that the magic of tonight was an illusion. He was going to take advantage of it as long as it lasted.

She turned to go to the dance floor, and Miguel felt as if someone had punched him in the stomach. Half of her dress was missing! At least, that's how it appeared at first glance. Somehow he'd only seen the front of her dress, and now that he'd seen how the dress revealed the long, elegant lines of her back, how the silken fabric fluttered delicately over her hips and down her legs, desire nearly incapacitated him. He made it to the dance floor just a few feet behind her, laboring with every step. He could delude himself all he wanted, but when Vicky turned to him, he knew this night was like no other. And she knew it, too. It would be their last one together. After this, their lives would change forever.

The music filled his mind as Vicky stepped into his arms and filled his senses. Nothing compared to the way they fitted together. He cupped her hand in one of his and placed his other one in the small of her back. There was nowhere to place his hand where he didn't touch her skin.

It was warm and soft and silky beneath his fingers, and he itched to drag his hand over every inch of her. He looked into her eyes and stepped into the music.

They didn't speak. They didn't have to. Vicky closed

her eyes and with a sigh pressed her temple against his jaw. Miguel nearly groaned. Every move, every sigh, every breath she took brought her closer to him, closer inside his heart.

The night moved forward and he didn't want to let go of her. The songs melted together the way he and Vicky melted together, until he received a tap on the shoulder, startling him out of his fantasy.

"Victoria, I believe you were going to save this particular dance for me." Mr. Hampton stood waiting with his wife, who looked at Miguel.

"Why don't we just switch partners for a few? That should shake things up a little." Mrs. Hampton held out her hand to him.

Unable to speak for the emotions strangling him, he simply nodded and made the change.

Victoria chatted with Thomas, but allowed her gaze to follow Miguel. He was such a handsome man and in a tux utterly delicious.

"He's quite the young man, isn't he?" Thomas asked with a knowing smile.

"Yes, he is." Vicky couldn't deny it. "Mother would have liked him."

"What does your father think?"

"Oh, he hasn't met Dr. Torres yet." The thought of it made Vicky cringe. When that happened, she'd likely need a sedative.

"Give you father a chance, Victoria. He might surprise you."

"That would be a novel experience."

"He only wants what's best for you."

"I know." It was his methods that Vicky didn't agree with, but that was an argument for another time.

Vicky didn't get to dance with Miguel any more, but she saw him dancing with Tilly. The woman looked so small and dainty compared to Miguel and she looked as if she was having a fabulous time in a silk-and-sequin dress that she had bought just for the event. Duties and small problems required Vicky's attention, and she kept her eye on Miguel as he made his way through the crowd, being drawn into conversations he probably didn't want to have.

She looked at him with pride pulsing in her chest. He smiled, he talked and he charmed everyone he came into contact with. Then the warmth in her chest was shoved away by an icy chill.

Miguel approached her father's table.

CHAPTER SEVENTEEN

Too late! She was too late! Her father was standing and holding his hand out to Miguel. From appearances, it was a friendly gesture, but her father measured a man by the strength of his handshake. Sometimes that was all it took to make or break a business deal.

"I hear good things about you and your clinic, Dr. Torres," Charles Sterling-Thorne said, and came around the table.

"Vicky…Victoria is being generous, I'm sure."

"Nonsense. She just put the idea out there. I do my own research before I put my money anywhere."

"And what did you find?" A muscle in Miguel's jaw twitched. She could see it from where she was, standing paralyzed, her heart racing as she watched the interaction between the two most important men in her life.

"Fabulous setup. You've taken a dying clinic and turned it around in just a few years. You should be proud of yourself."

Her eyes went wide, and her jaw went slack. A compliment from her father! Now she knew she needed that sedative.

Miguel grinned and the tension in his shoulders

eased. "Thank you. It's taken a lot of work, but I'm ready to move on now."

Tears filled her eyes at that statement. She was so proud of him.

"I'm certain there was more than a small sacrifice involved. With that kind of success there always is." He narrowed his eyes and gave Miguel a considering look. "Have you ever considered working in the wine industry?"

Miguel laughed. "No, sir. Medicine is where I need to be."

"You sound just like my daughter." He sighed.

The paralysis in her legs eased, and Vicky was finally able to move forward.

"Victoria, there you are, darling." Charles held out his arm to her, and she went to his side eagerly for the first time in a very long time. "You've put together a wonderful event here tonight."

"Thank you, Daddy. I see you've met Dr. Torres."

"Yes. And I have to say my money will indeed be well spent at your clinic."

"Thank you," she whispered, then pulled back. Losing control of emotions in front of Charles Sterling-Thorne was not something one did.

Edward stood and left his two companions at the table. "I believe the next dance is mine."

Vicky grinned. "Absolutely." Vicky looked at her father. "You behave yourself while I'm gone."

This time it was his jaw that dropped. "Me?"

She just grinned as Eddy led her away.

"I can't believe you said that," Eddy said.

"I can't believe I did either, but it felt good."

"I think our little Victoria has found her wings." He pulled her close and twirled her across the dance floor.

Miguel watched as Edward swirled and twirled Vicky. She was incredibly beautiful, and he knew he'd fallen for her. Despite all his reprimands to himself, he'd gone and done it.

"She's quite a beauty, isn't she?" Charles asked.

"Yes, she is. Inside and out."

"I'm finally beginning to see that." He sighed. "Congratulations, Dr. Torres. You've done fine things in your career, and I'm certain that you'll continue to do them in your future at University Hospital."

"Vicky mentioned it to you?" His brows twitched up at that.

His eyes glittered with amusement. "Research."

Miguel nodded. He was beginning to understand what Vicky had been talking about. There was no getting anything past Charles Sterling-Thorne.

Distracted with more conversations, he lost track of Vicky in minutes. Time seemed to move strangely this night, coming to a halt at precious moments and speeding by at others. Then Carlos and his parents approached.

"Hey, man. We're taking off. Mom's had enough fun for one night."

She gave him a playful glare. "Carlos is the one who needs to take it easy. He's been very active tonight and I don't want to him to have a relapse when he's been doing so well." She motioned for a hug and a kiss from Miguel, and he quickly obliged. "Thank you for a wonderful evening, *mijo*. Now go find your lady."

"My lady?"

"You know." She pulled back. "Good night." As they departed it seemed to be the beginning of a mass exodus, starting with the older folks. The younger ones would stay on the dance floor until the music stopped and they were shooed out of the ballroom.

His lady? Was that what Vicky was? Was that what he wanted her to be? He looked for Vicky and found her saying goodbye to several couples. What was it that she wanted? There was only one way to find out.

"Vicky?"

She turned toward him and he saw the fatigue in her. Although she stood straight and elegant, he knew her well enough now to know that she was exhausted.

"Are you leaving?" she asked, her eyes wide.

"No. I wanted to talk to you."

He took her elbow and walked with her to a side alcove where they could chat.

"Is something wrong?" she asked. "Seems like everyone had a good time and we've raised a boatload of money for the clinic."

"Yes, it's true. Thank you. Tonight could never have happened without you."

"I was happy to help out."

"Seems like I've gotten a lot out of tonight." He faced her, stepped a little closer to her and looked down into her eyes. Her pupils dilated a little and he knew he'd surprised her. "Is there anything you want out of tonight? Is there anything that you want?" That was as close as he could get at the moment to revealing the emotions that were about to swamp him. He'd hidden his feelings for so long that speaking them out loud wasn't possible at the moment.

A small gasp came from her, and then she took a deep breath, her gaze holding on to his. Carefully, she placed one of her hands on his arm, and the heat of her burned right through his sleeve. The air between them sparkled.

"I want tonight. I want you to hold me for one night. To pretend for just one night that there are no barriers between us. Nothing to hold us back. Just a man and a woman who might have cared about each other had the circumstances been different."

"Victoria," he said, his voice dark, husky, making her shiver. This was the first time he'd used her proper name. "I'll hold you tonight. I'll spend this night with you, make love to you, with you, because I want it, *and* you want it."

Her gaze flashed to him, wanting it to be true, hoping she'd not just imagined his words. If this was the end between them, she wanted to have everything out in the open. Raising her head and taking a deep, tremulous breath, she held her hand out to him. "I think I'm ready to leave, Dr. Torres. Will you join me upstairs?"

Without a word he took her hand in his and escorted her away from the crowd, the lights, the atmosphere that neither of them truly belonged in. In silence they walked away. With her hand still in his, he felt the tremors, the moisture of her palm, and knew she was as nervous, as excited as he was. Moments later, closed into the elevator with two other couples, he stood beside her, observing her statuesque, svelte form, and wondered how he had not seen the true Victoria. She had been everything then that she was now, just in different attire. Perhaps he hadn't wanted to see it. Perhaps he had chosen to close his eyes to what had been right in front of him the entire time she'd been working at the clinic. In the years he'd worked there he knew he had become more jaded, more disillusioned with life. Now he realized the depth of his despair if he had missed seeing the true Victoria in the simple clothes she'd hidden beneath.

After an interminable wait, the other couples got off the elevator at their floor and the doors slid closed silently, leaving them alone together. Trembling with need, with want, he turned his head and looked down at her.

There was nothing simple about Victoria Sterling-Thorne. She was the most gorgeous, compassionate, smartest woman he'd ever known, and he was an idiot for not recognizing what she was sooner.

Miguel didn't know how to feel, how to act, how to be inside. The knots in his stomach hadn't gone away all night, even though everything that had occurred was for the benefit of their clinic and the people in their community. He was humbled by the outpouring of support from people he didn't know and never would have turned to for help. All because of Vicky. Victoria.

With silence and sizzling tension between them, he escorted her out of the elevator and to her room. The hall was quiet, the dim lighting providing a smoky atmosphere where anything seemed possible. There was definitely magic in the air tonight.

"I'll…I'll just get the card…out of my purse." She didn't look at him, just opened her bag.

Without a word he watched her fumble with the silly little bit of fabric that could hardly be called a purse. Nothing more than lipstick and a key would fit in that thing. She had her back to him as she leaned toward the dim lighting.

Unable to avoid looking, unable to resist the temptation of her any longer, he allowed himself one long, lingering look at the silken length of her back, at what was revealed by the upsweep of her hair that bared the long, delicate curve of her neck. The hairpin decorated with diamonds that he hadn't noticed before twinkled like stars. The crisscrossed silken ties of the dress over her back revealed more of her than he'd ever seen and only whetted his appetite for more. He swallowed and tried to choke down the words that struggled to surface in him. He had to apologize, he needed to apologize. He'd been an idiot, but the words wouldn't come. Somehow, he would make it up to her. Somehow, he would make it right between them. Tonight.

"Dammit. It won't work," she said as she struggled with the key card.

He was just inches away and moved forward, placing his hand on her left thigh. She stilled instantly and stiffened, her breathing quick and shaky. Every sense he had was filled with her. "Shh. Shh. You have to take it slow, easy," he whispered close to her, and let his lips touch the outer curve of her ear, let the tip of his tongue trace the shape. She shivered, and didn't pull away from him. "Take it slow. Ease it in." In a precise move he placed his right hand over hers and guided the card into the narrow slot with a smooth movement of their hands joined together, and then pulled back with the same action.

Green light, a click and the door opened. With a ragged breath Vicky turned her face toward him and tilted it up, her eyes soft with the same want that raged inside of him. Her breath came in short pants, and she rested her head on his right shoulder.

"Miguel."

The whisper of her voice was a siren song that filled his mind, and he was powerless to resist the call. He felt the trembling muscles of her stomach, of her hips, as his fingers slid upward. Releasing her hand, he turned her face toward him and closed the gap.

As if knowing the moment had come between them, Vicky met his kiss with parted lips. Eager, anticipating, wanting. There was no longer any pretense between them. They wanted each other, and tonight was the night to bare secrets, souls and skin.

Clasping his arms around her, he brought her lithe body against him. Every curve, every line of her pressed against him as she answered his kiss. He cupped a hand against the back of her head while he plundered her mouth. Her tongue, soft and sweet, answered his call and desire raged through him. Somehow, he managed to walk them into the room before the lock snapped shut again. Turning with her, he pressed her against the door, trapping her with his body.

Vicky raised her arms and wrapped them around Miguel's neck. The feel of him against her was so strong, so right. Her heart thundered in her chest, and desire like she'd never known raced through her body. Tingles and memories of what her body wanted, what it could do, made her want Miguel naked. Now.

She pushed against the tux jacket and succeeded in getting his attention long enough to drop the thing to the floor. His hands ranged over her and then paused to cup her bottom, tipping her hips up against the heat and strength of his arousal. A groan caught in her throat.

Desire spiraled through her body, and moist heat flowed. The trembling inside grew as she cupped her hands around Miguel's face, pushing back slightly. "I want to undress you." She bit her lip. Such bold, wanton statements had never come from her. She was shy and an introvert, but with him aroused and wanting her so, shyness melted away to the truth. "I want to see you."

He planted a sweet kiss on her lips. "Are you positive you want this?" He looked at her, vulnerability that she'd never seen blatant in the warm eyes. "That you want this night and...me?" He swallowed.

She knew that she loved him, that the feelings in her heart were true. "I'm more sure than I've ever been about anything." She let her glance fall to his parted lips. His breath rushed in and out, and she felt the racing of his heart beneath her hand. He was as vulnerable as she.

With a groan, he pressed his lips to hers again, tugging and almost drawing her into him. Her trembling fingers released the cummerbund first then she turned her attention to the buttons of his shirt, releasing them one by one and revealing the smooth, tawny skin beneath. She shoved the shirt open. He was simply a beautiful man. And for this night he was hers.

Eyes watching her, ranging over her body, Miguel stepped back long enough to remove his shirt. And she swallowed, her mouth nearly watering at the sight of him. Casually, he reached for his waistband and released the catch, removed his shoes then socks.

"Oh, my." She stilled as nerves that she'd thought had fled returned in full force. What if she didn't please him? What if...? So many haunts of the past tried to return, but she focused on the want in Miguel's eyes, vowed to live in the moment and shoved away the past. She reached out to him, but he caught her hand and pressed a kiss to the palm, his gaze never leaving hers.

"My turn."

He reached for her shoulders and turned her away from him. The hot feel of his wet mouth on her bare shoulder nearly dropped her to her knees. He pressed his arousal against her bottom, his hands drawing her hips back. One hand ranged upward over her stomach, and paused at a breast, testing and teasing it. Then his mouth moved to her ear. "How do you get this dress off?"

"It's kind of complicated," she whispered, and looked up at him. Desire shone hot in his eyes.

"I see that. How did you get it on?" Another kiss to her shoulder made her shiver.

"With difficulty," she said, and pressed her forehead against his cheek, settling now into the feelings, the essence of him, allowing the pleasure of the moment to wash over her, savoring every nuance of the moment that she knew was never going to come again.

"Let me see what I can do."

He placed his hands on her thighs and began to bunch the dress up into his hands, drawing the silken material up her legs, revealing more and more of her body to him. Allowing him to touch her, to let himself have free access to her was a glorious feeling. He eased the material up over her bottom and then stilled.

"Is something wrong? Is it stuck?" she asked.

"Oh, no. Not at all." Seconds later he pulled the dress upward, and she raised her arms as he removed it completely. It landed on the floor with a light clatter of sequins and swoosh of silk. "A thong is a beautiful thing. Seeing you in one is even better." He sighed and let his hand stroke over her perfectly shaped bottom. "You have the loveliest curves I've ever seen."

Heat suffused her at the compliment and shyness fell away. She turned to face him, the moment of truth revealed. The desire to run, to cover herself, raged within her, but when she looked up at him she was paralyzed by the beauty of him as he looked at her. In that moment she was absolutely lost in him.

Miguel swallowed as he turned her around and took her hand. He wanted this woman with everything he had in him. Allowing his gaze to wander, he looked at her from head to toe, memorizing everything revealed to him, for him. Her hair remained up, a necklace of gems gleaming around her neck. Lovely, pink-tipped breasts stood high. The inner curve of her narrow waist, the slight roundness of her abdomen and the scrap of tiny fabric called a thong made his mouth water. Long, endless silky-smooth legs that he wanted wrapped around his hips tapered down to trim feet and high-heeled sandals. He held her hand and stepped back from her, seeing her, watching her, appreciating the beauty of her from shoes to smile.

"As long as I live, I will never forget this moment, this picture of you right now." He raised his gaze to hers, and his heart cramped from the beauty of all she was, inside and out. The anger, the resentment simply fell away from him. There was no place for it here tonight.

"Neither will I."

Unable to resist the temptation of her any longer and no longer willing to try, he moved in front of her, allowing her nipples to touch his chest. "I want to touch you, to taste you, to feel every inch of you against me."

"Yes." She reached for him, and he scooped her up

and carried her to the bed. Turning, he fell backward with her sprawled on top of him. As much as he adored it, the thong had to go, and he tugged the thing off her then shoved away the remainder of his own clothing.

With his hot skin against hers, Miguel pressed her back into the silken softness of the cool bedding. His mouth plundered her and left her breathless and wanting more. His hands were all over her, the light rub of calluses stirring her more than she'd thought possible.

He eased away and used that hot mouth of his to blaze a trail down her neck, over her collarbone and to her breast. Teasing and sucking her nipple, he held her captive as he pressed the hot length of his erection against her leg. Every sense in her soared to life as he touched and teased and tested her ribs, her abdomen, her hips.

Squirming beneath him, she wanted him trembling as much as she was. "Come here. I need you."

He raised his head and met her eyes. She dug her fingers into his hair. "Soon. Very soon," he whispered, and pulled away from her, continuing to kiss and lick and tease his way over her body. The inside of her ankle, the inside of her knee fell victim to his kisses and caresses. Her thighs fared the same as he made his way upward, pausing at the juncture to place hot, stirring kisses in each corner. When he opened his mouth over her core, she clutched the bedding and bit her lips together to stifle the scream in her throat.

The heat of his tongue traced over her tender woman's flesh, stirring her to heights she'd not known existed. Her body, stirred beyond comprehension, sizzled. When he eased a finger inside her, she crashed, her body no longer her own.

Then he was kissing her again and she held him tight, wanting to please him as much as he pleased her. He pulled back, breathless, and pressed his forehead against hers. "Are you on birth control?"

"No. Where's my purse?"

Turning, he looked around, then left the bed and returned with the tiny thing. "This won't help what I want to do."

She took it from him, extracted a condom and threw the purse across the bed. "This will." She tore the wrapping open and pulled out the little bit of magic inside.

"You came prepared," he said, and took it from her.

"No. I came with hope." With her hands over his, they eased the protective sheath down over him. "Love me," she said, and tears clouded her vision.

"I do," he whispered an instant before his mouth covered hers again.

The weight of him pressed her down, and she reveled in the textures and sensations of him against her, feeling delicate and protected all at once. He drew one of her knees up and eased it outward, giving him greater access. Her hands urged him on, and she tilted her hips up to receive him inside her.

Miguel pressed forward, the heat of him parting her flesh and filling her as far as he could go. This was the way love was supposed to be made.

He stilled, catching his breath, or the night was going to be over long before he intended. The feel of her hot flesh surrounding him, pressing on him, nearly made him cry out from the sheer pleasure of it.

Joined with her now, it was the most beautiful thing he'd ever experienced. Easing back, he wanted to prolong the pleasure for both of them. The pace he set was slow and designed for ultimate pleasure. When she locked her legs around his hips and squeezed, the time for slowness ended. He clasped her hips in his hands and fell hard into her, surging forward and back, letting his body take over, giving up any semblance of control.

Vicky dug her fingers into his upper arms, and she turned her face to the side. He pressed his mouth to her ear. "Don't hold it in. I want to hear you."

Turning back, she pressed her cheek to his and her breath warmed his skin. She gasped and clutched him tighter as her body responded to him again, and he lost all the control that he'd once thought he had.

Unable to suppress the wave that surged through him, he went with it, allowed it to take him under, and he drowned himself in the passion of the moment. Crying out his own pleasure, he held her tight as the final pulses of his body drifted away.

He rolled over, taking his weight off her, and, drawing her to his side, he held her against him.

CHAPTER EIGHTEEN

"ARE you okay?" he asked, and let his hand stroke its way down her back and over the curve of her hip.

"Oh, yeah. I'm good," she said, still marveling at the fire between them. Making love with Miguel was more than anything she'd imagined. "How about you?"

"I'm good, too." A sigh of contentment rolled out of him.

As his touch soothed her and stroked her skin she allowed herself to reciprocate and explored his chest and abdomen with her fingers. Intimacy with Miguel was an experience she'd never thought possible and here she was, right where she wanted to be. It was so much more than she'd hoped for.

They made love twice more and then showered together with strokes and sighs and kisses of desperation as their night of magic eased away with the breaking of dawn over the mountains.

"I guess this is it, then, isn't it?" she asked, tugging her robe more tightly around her. Though they'd recently left a very hot shower she felt cold and she hugged her arms around herself as she watched Miguel dress. The pain in her chest had begun when their last kiss had ended. It was over, and she knew it.

His jacket lay on the end of the rumpled bed with a bundle of envelopes sticking out of the inner pocket. That was the reason they were there, for the benefit of the clinic, not to satisfy her personal needs. The hope that she had come into this night with faded away. Even hope as strong as hers couldn't overcome some things.

"This has been a night I'll never forget." He pulled her closer and pressed a chaste kiss to her forehead. In a hurried movement he picked up his jacket and left the suite. The snap of the door closing shut ended any chance for a reconciliation between them. It was final.

Exhausted and anguished, she somehow made the drive home and brought her belongings in from the car, but dropped the suitcase by the front door and left it there. There was no name for the type of pain and numbness that overwhelmed her.

Although she'd left her cottage not twenty-four hours ago, it felt and smelled stale, as if a lifetime had passed. She opened several windows to catch the breeze from the river. Dressed in shorts, a plain shirt and flimsy sandals, she grabbed a bottle of water and her cell phone, and headed out to the vineyard.

This was her solace, where she would find the peace she needed, and hopefully the strength to go on after knowing what a night with Miguel was like, knowing she'd never have it again. After the past month of working and planning for the event, she was exhausted. She felt like Cinderella on the day after the ball. At least the event had been a wild success and Miguel would be able to move on knowing that the clinic was as solvent as it could be.

Her path seemed meandering, but it led her eventually to the bench swing that was tucked away in a secret part of the vineyard. She sat and put the swing into motion then tucked her legs beneath her, hoping the motion would soothe her battered soul.

The soft sounds of the breeze, the birds nesting in the nearby trees, the swish of the horses as they chased flies with their tails, all melded together in one blissful symphony of nature.

Then the tears came. In the privacy of her vineyard she allowed herself to let go and ease the tension that had been building in her for months. She loved Miguel, but now she was more certain than ever that there would be nothing between them. Last night had proved that. They'd shared a beautiful experience and then walked away from each other. Letting go was always painful. Being in such a beautiful, peaceful place helped. Only time would ease the pain, but she would never, ever forget him.

She'd had relationships in the past, but the breakups had never hurt her the way this one did. Not even her divorce had been this painful. Eventually, she calmed down and reconnected with the sounds of peace around her until the sound of footsteps on dirt penetrated her focus. One of the horses must have gotten out and decided to have a stroll through the vines. Wouldn't her father have a fit if that happened? She opened her eyes and down the row in front of her she found the source of the disturbance, and it wasn't a horse.

Miguel stood there.

Or perhaps against the afternoon sun the image was an illusion, a lame attempt by her heart to console her. Denial was a very powerful part of the grieving process. She knew that, but to have the full-blown figure of Miguel approaching her was something else. She blinked several times then held a hand up to shade the sun from her eyes. Nope. That was definitely Miguel getting closer to her, not an illusion. She swallowed and her heart pounded loud in her ears.

"What are you doing here?" She rubbed her hands over her face and dashed away any lingering moisture, but she was certain her face was red and puffy. He would notice.

"I needed to take a walk. I was restless." He shoved his hands down into the pockets of his khaki shorts and looked down at the ground then back up at her with an intensity that surprised her.

The nerves in the pit of her stomach clenched. What was he talking about? "There are plenty of places to walk in this town. There are the sidewalks, the parks, the Nature Center, the path down by the river." The implication was clear. Why here?

"I like this stretch of the river, but it's on private property, you know."

She stepped forward. "I know."

"I wanted to come ask one of the owners if I could take a walk here, in the vineyard." He stopped in front of her, just a foot away, and looked down at her, his eyes unreadable with the sun behind him. "I wanted to ask if she'd go along for a very long walk with me."

"Miguel, what are you talking about? What are you doing here?" She was so tired and confused she didn't know what to think, couldn't process what he was telling her.

He took her hand and led her back to the swing she had just left. They sat. "Leaving you this morning was the hardest thing I've ever had to do." He took her hands in his and squeezed. "That feeling, that pain, is something I never want to experience again." He cleared his throat and swallowed a few times. "This is so hard to say."

"I know. When you left and didn't look back, I knew things were over for us."

"Then when I thought of a future, I couldn't think of one without you in it, but I don't think I can do this." He raised a hand and indicated the mansion and vines.

"We don't need to do this. In fact, we need to do something else entirely. There's something you ought to know. Growing up in this environment was difficult and I know that's hard for some people to understand. I had few friends, no boyfriends through school because the boys I knew were afraid of my father. Then people only wanted to know me because of my name and my family's money." She shuddered and heaved out a trembling sigh. "The only thing I have of my own is my nursing career." Leaning her head back against the swing, she closed her eyes briefly. "Going to nursing school was the only time I've ever held my own against my father. Until now. Now I have a career and a job I love. Working at the clinic means everything to me, and I've discovered that I'm so much more capable than I've ever thought. It's because of the clinic. Because of you, Miguel."

"My past, my brother's death has haunted me through my life. I never told you but I was engaged when Emilio was killed."

"No, I didn't know that." Compassion for the young man that he had been welled in her. He'd been so hurt by life at a young age and had only survived without caving in to the grief because of his personal strength, strength he didn't even know he had.

"When I didn't recover from Emilio's death, she

broke things off. I couldn't give her what she needed and things just fell apart between us." He placed an arm on the back of the swing and teased her hair with his fingers.

"As you know, I'm divorced. It was a mistake from the start." She sighed and allowed the pain of her past to bubble up. "He was after connections with my family and the business. I was incidental to the relationship." Though it pained her to say it, it was the truth.

He froze as the white-hot heat of protectiveness struck him. "No one should be incidental in a relationship. You are precious and the man was a total idiot for not seeing it." As soon as the words left his mouth, he wondered if that was a statement about himself. "I should have seen it soon, too, Vicky. I'm sorry." He sighed and dropped his gaze. "I'm guilty of not seeing the real you in the beginning, too. But you've helped me to heal from Emilio's death and to learn to put the past behind me."

"You won't ever forget Emilio, but you can let go of the pain surrounding him." He'd begun the process and maybe some small part of that was due to her help. "If I've helped in any way, I'm very glad."

"I think from here we need to make a vow that the future is ours and one that we make together. One that's our own."

She gasped, uncertain what he meant and not wanting to jump to conclusions. Did he mean at the clinic, to go to the hospital with him? What? Her heart raced and her mouth went dry. "Tell me what you mean by that."

Miguel squeezed her hands then dropped to the dirt in front of her. "Last night was filled with more magic and passion than I have a right to, but I don't want to let go of it, or let go of you." He placed his hands on her thighs. "I don't know what my future is going to hold, but I want you in whatever that is. I want us to build one together." He looked down at his hands then back up at her. "I don't know when or where, and there are probably a dozen reasons why you shouldn't, but, Victoria Sterling-Thorne, will you marry me?"

She launched herself from the swing with a squeal and wrapped her arms around his shoulders. Unprepared for the sudden weight of her, Miguel toppled over, and they crashed to the ground. She spread kisses over his face and ended with one long, hot kiss that left them both breathless.

"Is that a yes?" he asked when he could breathe again.

"Yes, that's a yes."

He hugged her tight. "Oh, good. If that had been a no, I was going to get worried."

They sat up and returned to the swing where Vicky curled against Miguel's side and they exchanged kisses that got longer and longer and nearly as hot as the sun overhead.

"How did you find me out here?" She pulled back with a frown.

"I stopped at the house."

"You did?" Her stomach clenched.

"Your father told me you'd probably be out here." Miguel winked. "He's actually not so bad when you get to know him a little."

This was a day of miracles if Charles was being civilized. "You actually spoke to my father?"

"Yes, when I told him I wanted to marry you."

Stunned, Vicky stared at him. "I love you."

"I love you right back."

EPILOGUE

VICKY looked at the schedule on Miguel's computer. There were too many holes in the physician side, but at least they were getting filled in one by one.

She grinned. Two months ago she'd never have imagined so many changes in the clinic. Now they seemed natural. With some additional brainstorming with Dr. Flemming, who had indeed taken over nearly half of Miguel's shifts, they had found extra physicians to put in time so that Miguel could in good conscience accept the position at University Hospital.

"Got a minute?" Tilly asked from the doorway.

"Sure. Come on in." Vicky sipped from her coffee cup. "How's Carlos doing on the computer?"

"Not too bad for a beginner," Tilly said, and grinned.

They'd made some changes in staffing. Since Carlos was officially on light duty, Tilly had trained him to take over the computer scheduling and answering phones so that her nursing skills could be better utilized triaging patients. Vicky was now the office manager and had given most of her duties over to Tilly.

"I'm just glad he could come back at all."

"There are a few things I wanted to ask you about.

You may have done things differently when you were triaging, but I just wanted to see if this change is okay with you."

Although Tilly was the triage nurse and Vicky now the office manager, they had an equal relationship and interest in the clinic. "Let's see it." They looked over Tilly's proposed changes and Vicky had no issues with them. "Looks good. If something doesn't work, we can always try something else, right?"

"Sure. Just like always."

The phone rang and Tilly left as Vicky returned to her scheduling.

Hours had passed when she felt a presence in the doorway. When she looked up, her heart flipped and a smile crossed her face. "Hi, there. What are you doing here?"

Miguel crossed the room and leaned on the desk beside her. "It's quitting time. Got time for dinner?"

"Sure. Anything special?"

"I think it is. We're celebrating."

"I know I got most of the schedule filled, but is it worthy of a celebration?" She smiled.

"Not that—this." He placed two fingers in his shirt pocket and fished out a small wrapped package. Holding it in the palm of his hand, he waited for her to take it.

"Ooh. I see." She licked her lips. "I can't take it now."

"What?"

"I'm in work clothes at the end of the day. I should be wearing a dress and—"

"You were in work clothes when I met you and they don't detract at all from the way I feel about you."

"Miguel," she whispered, and tears filled her eyes.

"I love you." Carefully, she took the box from his hand, unwrapped it and opened it. Her first sight of the ring made her breath hitch. "It's gorgeous."

"I hope it fits." He extracted it from the box and placed it on the tip of her finger. "Victoria Sterling-Thorne, will you do me the honor of being my wife sometime very soon?"

"I will."

He pushed the ring all the way onto her finger and it fit to perfection—just the way they fit together.